THE WOLF OF WESTMORE

REGENCY ROGUES
BOOK THREE

AMALIE HOWARD

*For my wonderful readers
who asked for this story*

CHAPTER 1

ENGLAND, 1822

Lady Jocelyn Capehart, daughter of the dour Duke of Tyne, peered at her reflection and let out a pleased exhale. Covered in a crimson cloak, her sunset-red hair hidden under a dark wig, and her face painted in a way that accentuated her features, she was mostly unrecognizable. Because for what she intended to do tonight, she had to be.

No one could connect her back to her father. The duke was cruel enough to lock her in a convent and throw away the key until he could use her as a pawn in some marriage to bolster his influence or his holdings. Three daughters...and each one of them disposable. Two already married off and only she remained. Jocelyn was determined to avoid the same fate as her older sisters, though she knew her prospects were out of her hands.

Unless she did something about it first.

She wanted to live—to experience some of the world—before she was forced to marry a man three times her age and deliver his blue-blooded heirs for the sake of her father's ambition. And she knew that was what Tyne had planned. The Marquess of Perrin was an old lecher of a man whose property adjoined theirs to the east. The thought of sharing a marriage bed with him made her want to retch.

Jocelyn bit her lip and balled her trembling hands. Inviting ruination was one thing, but scandal had a way of corrupting everything. She did love her family, despite her parents' iron fists where she, and her precious virtue, were concerned. While she craved escape from the chains of duty, she didn't want to bring shame down upon them. Hence all her subterfuge.

With luck, her daring adventure would remain a wonderful, enduring secret to tide her through an inevitably bleak future.

"You can do this," she said to herself, pursing crimson-stained lips that made them seem fuller, and reached for the reticule that lay on the top of the dresser. She pulled out a plain black, gold-dusted invitation and gulped. A scandalous invitation to an auction at the most notorious club in England, part owned by Wulfric Bane, the Duke of Westmore.

The name made a frisson course through her. Would she see him tonight?

She hadn't seen the master of the ducal estate across the river in years. Their properties were separated by the River Tyne—a wide swatch of dangerous water that embodied the churning relationship between their families, from their competing shipping and mining businesses to their lands and influence in Northumberland and Durham.

The family rivalry went as far back as the Middle Ages. If there was ever any peace between them, it was never recorded in any history books, to Jocelyn's knowledge. The Capeharts were always taught to loathe the Banes, and vice versa, and the contention had endured through the ages. If there was ever a dispute, they were always on opposing sides. If one liked oranges, the other would almost invariably like apples.

Although it was more about fortune and land than fruit these days.

Jocelyn had no idea what Westmore looked like now. She'd seen him from afar during her come-out in London years ago. He'd been rangy and formidable even then, a scowling presence in a corner of the ballroom, warning all and sundry away. And yet, she had been fascinated. The monster from all the stories her siblings told—the *Wolf* of Westmore.

It hadn't been fear that had tumbled through her as her eyes had greedily taken in the dark unruly hair, the thick layer of matching scruff on that hard jaw, and the glint in those predatory eyes, even from across an entire room...it had been a bolt of pure, unmitigated lust. And then, when that predacious gaze had met hers, spearing her like the trembling prey she was, Jocelyn hadn't been able to breathe.

That memory was engraved onto her brain.

Westmore had prowled toward her, lean and lithe, his piercing stare never wavering as he cut through the throng of guests. With each step, Jocelyn's body had locked, her knees wobbling beneath the sparkling new flounces of her gown, her pulse fluttering like a bird trapped in a bush, but she hadn't moved. She had remained still, held captive by a fiery orange-brown gaze that blazed with power and possession, until he stood a foot away.

"Who are you?" The demand had been uncouth, low and blunt, the sound of his voice like stones falling through silk. They had not even been introduced, but the Duke of Westmore obviously didn't care for social niceties, given the whispers and the gasps.

"Lady Jocelyn, Your Grace," she had replied.

His eyes had narrowed. "Tyne's girl?"

The hint of disgust had been plain as day to see, and Jocelyn had lifted her chin. "The Duke of Tyne's daughter, yes." She'd bristled with instant ire. He wasn't that much older than she, perhaps a little more than a handful of years, and yet he acted like she was a green miss fresh out of the schoolroom. "And perhaps you will find it polite to share who *you* are, considering that you stalked all the way over here and demanded my identity in such an unchivalrous manner?"

Heavy, dark slashes of eyebrows had climbed

with each scathing word. "You already know who I am," he drawled. "You addressed me as Your Grace."

Blast it, she had. Heat had crept into her cheeks, but she refused to cower. "Clearly my error, sir. I mistook you for someone else. A *gentleman* to whom I'd already been introduced, perhaps."

The set-down hadn't gone unnoticed, but a pair of vexingly full lips had twitched with mild amusement, eyelids hooding in a way that made her pulse scatter. "Then allow me to correct my *faux-pas*. Duke of Westmore, mortal enemy of the Capeharts."

"Not *my* mortal enemy," she'd replied with a cool half-smile. "At least not yet. I allow a gentleman to prove himself before committing him to be hanged, drawn, and quartered."

A spark of interest had lit the stare that had dropped to her lips, but then her best friend Prudence had come back from the retiring room and barreled into the duke's arms with a very unladylike squeal. "Wulfric, you're here!"

Wulfric. His given name suited him, Jocelyn had thought.

Wolfish, deadly, and singular.

"Look at you, my lady," the duke had rumbled in a light tone that had been a far cry from his previous hard one. "Roth didn't tell me you had grown this beautiful—for good reason, probably. Whom do I have to kill in this ballroom?"

Jocelyn's heart had shriveled at the obvious

affection between them, while Prudence had made a scoffing noise. "No one." She'd grinned. "Have you met my dearest friend in the world? Lady Jocelyn and I went to finishing school together."

Thick-lashed tawny eyes had drilled into hers. "I'm well aware of exactly who she is."

"Goodness, Wulfric," Prudence had muttered. "Isn't it time you let all that hostility go? Jocelyn isn't like her papa or her cousin or any of them. Give it a rest."

"Old habits die hard."

It was true. Their families had waged wars over old habits.

Over old everything.

After he'd escorted Prudence to the next waltz, Jocelyn had watched them dance with no small amount of envy, even though her own partner was more than charming. That had been the last time she'd seen the snarling excuse for a duke. Prudence had confided sadly that he'd gone back to the Continent. That season had been a whirlwind, before tragedy had struck. Prudence's shocking death had sent Jocelyn into mourning after that, and she had never returned to London, preferring to stay in the country.

Sometimes she wondered if Prudence's death had hit Westmore as hard as it had hit her. They'd been close, perhaps even someone that her best friend might have carried a secret tendre for. Jocelyn had seen the duke briefly at the funeral—a stark shadow of a man looming on the periphery—but never anywhere in the years after. She'd heard talk of him, of course. The Westmore name was synonymous with profanity in her household, especially when income and tenants were lost to her father because of him.

Scoundrel! Reprobate! Villain!

Westmore was everything her father hated… and everything she needed.

Nerves alight, Jocelyn turned over the invitation in her hand. It was addressed to her cousin Tybalt, and one he would never accept. She expected that it was sent as a barb—an invitation to a scandalous auction at the hottest social club in London, The Silver Scythe. Her cousin would never go, of course, not to a club owned by their family's most hated foe. But to her it was a ticket to freedom. At least for one night.

And if she only had one night, she intended to go out with a bang.

Quite literally.

CHAPTER 2

Wulfric Bane, the very smug Duke of Westmore, tugged his cravat off in the middle of The Silver Scythe as he came off the stage with a satisfied grin. It had already been scandalously untied to show more of his bared throat during the auction. The ladies had loved it—a little rule-breaking, for gents garbed in proper attire drove them wild and loosened the drawstrings on their reticules. Speaking of, he should probably locate the one who had won a night of his company to the tune of two-and-a-half thousand pounds.

Lady J.

He wondered who she was. Female guests used all kinds of names at the club for anonymity, especially when participating in an auction of the *ton's* most coveted gentlemen. At least it hadn't been Lady Darcy, a popular *nom de guerre*, thanks to an anonymous, irreverent periodical for ladies that was taking town by storm. He had his suspicions as to the identity of the outrageous author…but that mystery would be unraveled in its own time.

Matteo, the Marquess of Roth's man of affairs, attired in black trousers, a red banyan, and nothing but gold paint on his chest, had led the auction to delighted chaos. The rake loved the attention, not that Matteo cared at the moment. His interest was currently shared by a handsome young footman as well as a notorious widow who loved to draw nubile young men.

The last year, Roth, his business partner and half owner of The Silver Scythe, had won by a landslide to be a nude model for the very same dowager, Lady Hammerton. It had been hilarious in the extreme and Wulfric took great pleasure in ribbing the marquess about it. This time, however, Roth had been won by his wife, the dauntless marchioness who was intent on shaking up her husband's life. It was about time, Wulfric thought. Those two were perfect for each other—they simply needed to get out of their own way to realize it.

With any luck, they were doing just that in the offices upstairs.

Roth was hopelessly in love with his wife, though he couldn't see past his own nose when it came to her. But the bond between them was obvious, even to a man as jaded as Wulfric. Such a thing wasn't in the cards for him, however. Love was Pandora's box, which he intended to keep firmly shut. He was focused on his own lands and cheating the Duke of Tyne out of any opportunity. That reminded him. The dukedom was thriving in Durham, but it was about time Wulfric upped the stakes. He intended to drive the man to ruin.

For now, however, he had to find his auction winner.

Lady J. He'd been pleasantly surprised at the small fortune—two-and-a-half thousand pounds. Roth had looked astonished, too, eyes widening with what looked like recognition in the direction of the bidder, but Wulfric knew it was more likely due to the exorbitant amount. He'd thought he'd had the highest bid in the bag until Roth had been won by his wife for double that. The bastard had the devil's own luck.

Wulfric wondered if *his* winner was comely. The hint of a profile in the crowd had been enough to convince him that she might be. Not that it mattered. He enjoyed all females, especially ones with a little bit of wit and salt about them. Most of the female members of The Silver Scythe were smart and capable, and not afraid to let the world know it. While he was a dominant lover, he wasn't above letting a woman take the reins once in a while, if so inclined.

Though the club catered to more dissolute appetites, the famed bachelor auction wasn't only about sex, though carnal relations weren't off the table. If such desire was mutually consensual, and it had to be, the couple could avail themselves of one of the many private suites scattered throughout the labyrinthian space. While the auction itself flirted with scandal, all the proceeds went to charity. The latter was in

Prue's name, no less. Wulfric let out a small chuckle. Prudence would have adored this hedonistic circus. It had been years since her death, and he still thought about her every day.

He suspected his best mate and Prue's brother, Roth, thought they had been involved, but his feelings for Prudence Vance went much deeper than anyone knew, even Roth. Some secrets belonged in the grave, and this was one of them. Wulfric rubbed at his aching chest, the hollow there taunting him of his own guilt. If only he could have saved Prudence from the fortune-hunting scum who had dragged her down with him in an opium den in Seven Dials, Prue might still be alive, but Wulfric hadn't been there.

He'd failed her. They'd all failed her.

And it was Tyne's fault.

Then again, Wulfric could have done a lot of things differently himself. Taken her under his wing as he should have. Protected her. Cherished her. Kept her safe.

Clearing his tight throat, he let out an uneven breath. He could not change the past, no matter how much he might wish to. Burying the memories back where they belonged, Wulfric strode through the club, eyes panning the throng searching for a spot of scarlet. It was crowded, and he still needed to find his winner. God only knew what the lady would expect of him.

Some of them requested for him to escort them to various parties—to be seen on the arm of the Duke of Westmore sparked both interest and competition—and one or two had opted for other sensual comforts. Thankfully, unlike Roth, he was unmarried and not bound by wedlock. And anything went, as long as it was in safe, mutually agreeable, *consensual* fun.

Consent was sovereign within the walls of The Silver Scythe.

His breath stilled in his throat when a diminutive figure in a red cloak and a matching red mask that covered most of her face cut boldly into his path. "Looking for me, Your Grace?"

Good God, but her voice was husky and rich, the lush low sound of it arrowing straight to his groin. Wulfric wished he could see her face, but perhaps she could be coaxed to remove the mask once they were in private. "Lady J, I presume," he drawled, hiding his unexpected reaction behind cool ennui. "As a matter of fact, I was."

"Well, here I am," she said softly.

"Here you are indeed."

Bloody hell, he sounded like a simpleton. Wulfric blinked, taking her in. She was petite, barely reaching his chest, the wealth of midnight-black hair coiffed in intricate loops adding an inch or two to her diminutive stature. Her crimson cloak or cape, or perhaps it was a new kind of fashionable costume, was made of voluminous satin, teasing along the subtle curves of her body and falling to the floor.

Body heating, his very interested stare swept

back up. Ribbons securing the cloak at her throat dropped down into her ample décolletage, the creamy skin there flushed. A pulse fluttered at the base of her neck, his gaze climbing to a pointed chin, parted red-stained lips, and a pair of glittering eyes of indeterminate color behind the mask.

"Do I pass muster, Your Grace?" she asked with a low throaty chuckle.

Wulfric faltered at the teasing, realizing that he'd been ogling her, but something about her ticked his brain. They'd met before—he was sure of it. But then again, he'd met many women over the years and at the club, especially. Normally, he was good with faces, but hers was well covered, so he would have to figure out the puzzle another way.

He gave an unabashed wink. "Would you like to return the favor, my lady? Evaluate and rank my individual assets?"

"Alas, Westmore, I already have the measure of you. The ladies call you the Duke of Bad Decisions, do you know? *Their* bad decisions." A pink tongue darted out to moisten her lips as more color climbed down the distractingly long column of her throat. He wondered how low that flush descended...whether it led to even rosier nipples. His mouth watered with a raw desire to taste them, to bite them until she whimpered. "It was why I bid on you, after all."

"What do you wish of me then? Dinner? A dance?" He paused for a beat. "More?"

The tempting little vixen tucked her arm in

his, and Wulfric couldn't help noticing how well her small body fit into his side, despite their marked difference in height. He was a tall man and she fit like she'd been made to be tucked into him. *Shielded* by him.

Wulfric frowned, confused by the arbitrary thought. Women who frequented The Silver Scythe didn't require protection—they were usually forces of nature, out for whatever bit of mischief they desired. He shook his head and discarded the random emotion. A lady who spent such a fortune on a gentleman's company wasn't looking for security; she was looking for something much more specific.

"I find myself suddenly interested in hearing what *more* entails," his companion said. "Perhaps you can give me a tour of your club and we can go from there?"

"As my lady wishes," he replied.

His companion might seem confident and bold, but he had a feeling that *Lady J* was playing a game meant for a more experienced woman. Or perhaps that was part of her allure...the innocent jade combination she had going for her. Dress and voice of a courtesan, eyes and mannerism of an ingenue. But Wulfric had learned over the years never to underestimate women, especially those who had the wherewithal to brave a club meant for vice and pleasure.

The Silver Scythe was an enormous maze, and it took them the better part of an hour before they'd ambled through it all, from the reception hall that led into the enormous gilded ballroom, to the gaming rooms with their felted tables and the dining rooms with rich, mahogany furniture and gold-framed paintings of bucolic scenes. They paused in the stocked library and writing rooms that had caught her fancy before moving on to the communal billiards and cigar lounges that welcomed both sexes, an art gallery that featured works of the club's members, the exercise and fitness center, and lastly, a number of private parlors for quiet conversation.

"That was the first floor," Wulfric said, when they got back to where they had started near the grand, curving staircase. "Up there are additional salons, as well as suites and rooms for guests."

He summoned a footman with a glass of champagne. "The whole place is incredible," she said, after a cautious sip. "I admit, I've never been to a social club before, especially one that welcomes women. Do you have many female members?"

"Several dozen," he replied, cataloging the information she shared without meaning to. It was more apparent by the minute that she was a lady of quality. One couldn't be sure if guests were from the beau monde or the demimonde. Sometimes a woman claimed the title of lady when they weren't part of the peerage, but Wulfric suspected that Lady J might very well be an aristocrat. Her mannerisms were too precise, her diction too crisp. She was clearly accustomed to luxury as well as the deference those of elevated station enjoyed. "Most prefer anonymity, but some do not. We also do not differentiate by station. As long as you can afford the fee and accept the rules, the doors are open."

"Rules?"

"The hard and fast rules are permission and consent, especially in the more…risqué areas of the club."

She blinked up at him, nearly gasping as her sip went down the wrong way. Her eyes flicked to the upper rooms as though expecting to see something scandalous on the landing. "Risqué?"

"Not up there. Going down is much more fun." His grin was slow and dangerous, her eyes widening at his obvious innuendo, before he pointed to another staircase behind them that led downstairs. "There's a lot more to the club on the lower levels."

Her throat worked. "What is there?"

"It's not for the faint of heart."

The underlying meaning—*not for someone like you*—was more than obvious.

She swung back to glare at him, those eyes— a warm bottle green now that he could see them in the light of the nearest wall sconce—flashed with ire. "You do not know me so well, Your Grace, to make such a judgment about the proficiency of my heart. Trust me, I can take whatever your little den of pleasure has to spare."

Christ, every dominant part of him rose to the challenge; he wanted to crowd into her space, take those saucy lips with his, and give her a taste of the hazards that existed below-stairs. But he also sensed that beneath all that bravado was a thread of uncertainty. Wulfric frowned. How had she procured an invitation? It was something he would have to bring up with Roth. They did their best to monitor the exclusive invitations, especially to non-members for the auction, but a few often got out. Case in point.

"Do you have your invitation, Lady J?" he asked.

An unreadable stare met his. "The factotum took it when I arrived. Is there a problem?"

He knew for a fact that Matteo would not have, which made it all the more suspicious. But it was done now, and she *had* contributed an immense sum for him. The least he could do was oblige, but first he needed to be sure that no fathers or brothers were going to come bashing down his door. "The age of majority is one-and-twenty. Are you above that?"

That pointy chin hiked. "I am three-and-twenty. How old are *you*?"

"Older than that. Are you here of your own free will?"

"I am." Those pretty red lips compressed slightly, something shadowy like worry appearing in her gaze before it disappeared as quickly as it had arrived. Determination and renewed resolve swallowed her irises. *Curious.* She eyed him and drained the contents of her glass in one gulp. "Are you done with the questions or shall I ask for my generous settlement to be returned?"

"Buyer's remorse?" he drawled, leaning back onto the balustrade.

The imperious little minx turned the tables on him and tossed her head. "I did not pay a fortune to be coddled and talked to death."

"What, pray tell, were you expecting?"

Stormy green eyes crashed into his. "Less talk, more action, Your Grace. In other words, more prick and less prejudice."

His mouth went slack, even as he wanted to laugh at her wit. Whatever he'd expected her to say, it was not that, at least not uttered so baldly by a woman he was starting to realize wasn't at all what she seemed. Perhaps she *wasn't* such an ingenue. Because by God, she was turning him into a mincing prude and he owned the bloody place.

"I beg your pardon?" he grunted.

"That's more like it. The begging. I've heard rumors that you're quite marvelous on your knees." The unnerving temptress gave him a half-smile that tugged at his memory, but for the life of him he could not place it. He could not *think*! Her provocative words were scrambling his brain, and all the blood in his body was rushing to his cock. "Your reputation precedes you in these anointed circles, do you know? Your skills in bed sport. If we are plain-speaking, I wish for you to educate me thoroughly, Westmore. Now will you show me downstairs, or shall I request another, more enthusiastic partner?"

Stunned practically senseless, Wulfric stared

at her. "Are you certain that this is what you want?"

"Don't ask me that again. Tonight is mine, and I intend to enjoy every second of it without reality crashing in. Allow me the fantasy, Your Grace. That is what I'm here for."

Wulfric understood that all too well...the need for escape.

"Very well, my lady. Your wish is my command. Welcome to the Underground."

CHAPTER 3

D ear Lord, she was going to lose her
virginity in a dungeon.
      With a very scary dungeon master.
   A very sultry, muscular, virile specimen who
made her body respond in ways she had not
known it could. Jocelyn peered up at him.
Goodness, he was huge, towering over her like a
silent warrior god. She was certain he could
pick her up with one hand. Her pulse streamed
at the notion of being manhandled by him...of
those huge palms fondling her overheated, un-
tried body, placing her where he wanted, however he wanted.

   Jocelyn went dizzy at the thought. She'd
planned this meticulously for months. Years, if
she was being honest with herself. Not the club,
the *man*. By her choice, the Duke of Westmore
was going to be her first. She was going to get
him out of her head once and for all, and see if
the reality matched up to the million-and-one
fevered dreams she'd had of him in every imag-

inable sexual position. Because while she was an innocent in body, she was extraordinarily fertile of mind and she wanted to try everything she'd envisioned.

Every wicked thing.

Her core fluttered, adding to more warmth between her legs.

Her parents might have plans for her future, but her body was hers. When the opportunity at The Silver Scythe had presented itself, Jocelyn had not hesitated. She had hoarded her pin money for years, and when she learned of the auction and that Westmore was one of the gentlemen up for bids, she'd sold two sets of expensive parure that her parents had gifted her for her birthdays. She'd come to the club with three thousand pounds in the form of a promissory note and a mission to be deflowered by one man.

The Duke of Westmore.

"So what do you think?" his deep voice asked, breaking her from her thoughts.

Jocelyn blinked and took in the sumptuous space. Like the floor above, no expense was spared, though the ambiance was much darker and richer. This space was designed for carnal pleasure. The furniture was over-stuffed and crafted for comfort, and the paintings on the walls of lewd, sensual scenes of cavorting nymphs and nude lovers made her blood run unspeakably hot. Everything in here was meant to seduce.

Flexible young ladies folded their beautiful

bodies into impossible shapes from hoops dangling from the ceiling. Jocelyn gaped up at them, gasping when one completed a particularly daring twist, the scrap of gold fabric between her thighs hiding nothing. Shirtless servants in golden silk breeches carried gilded trays to the guests lounging in the corners, whose eyes were fixed upon the performance above.

Gentlemen had partners of any sex perched on their laps while ladies leaned against other women, fingers interwoven and lips touching. Cravats and bodices were askew. If Jocelyn looked or listened closely, she'd catch a glimpse of an exposed breast or the sound of a ragged moan and the rasp of skin on skin. She imagined more than one gloveless hand skating up bare legs. The idea excited her unbearably. Some of these guests here, unlike the ones upstairs, did not wear masks. Likely because they did not care or were longtime members.

Jocelyn reached up to tug on the lace edge of hers.

"Wish to remove that?" Westmore asked, a hint of humor in his tone.

She shook her head. "No."

His intake of breath was soft. She knew he wanted to know who she was, but she also knew that the moment he realized the truth, all of this would be over. Jocelyn intended to be well and truly ruined before he had any inkling of her identity, if at all. Her mouth firmed with renewed purpose. She was doing this for herself... to know the touch of a man she had chosen of her own free will *and* to reduce the ills of being traded off like a precious prize to the decrepit Marquess of Perrin.

If her virtue was lost, perhaps he wouldn't want her.

One could only hope.

"What are those rooms?" she asked, noticing a row of clear glass windows over what she realized was the far end of a massive foyer. All the other secret nooks and crannies led from this main entry room. This was quite beyond anything she'd ever imagined.

"Those are for the guests who wish to watch but not participate. Shall we?"

Nodding with eagerness, she took his arm. When they reached the closest of the glass panes, Jocelyn's breath caught in her throat. In the first section, a woman dressed in black leather breeches and a black lace corset, stood over a gentleman strapped to a wooden contraption. Arms were tied above his head and his legs were spread. It was the most shockingly erotic position Jocelyn had ever seen, and for a heartbeat, it wasn't hard to imagine herself in the man's place.

She flinched when the leather fronds of the woman's whip whistled upward and hurtled down to mark his already reddened skin, though he did not look pained. In fact, he wore a look of intense euphoria. After a few well-placed strikes, the woman halted in her work, gloved fingers feathering down the man's sides and reaching around to the front of his hidden groin. A lewd moan escaped his lips as she caressed him, the pumping motion of her arm leaving no doubt as to what she was doing. A shiver of delight crept down Jocelyn's spine and spread into molten ripples between her hips. The scene was utterly wicked...and equally arousing.

"Come," Westmore commanded, and she wasn't sure whether it was an order for her body to release its maddeningly building tension or to follow him. She bit back a wild giggle and did the second.

In the next room, which featured a dais with an enormous bed, a woman lay on plump pillows and satin bedclothes while she was being tended to by four scantily dressed men, who rubbed her barely clothed body with oil. One pair smoothed slow glistening circles at her ankles and her knees, moving leisurely up her thighs, while the other two near her shoulders, kneaded her bare breasts. Jocelyn gasped and pinned her lips between her teeth. She was very aware of Westmore at her side, though she was sure that he was more than used to such scenes.

She glanced up, only to find him staring down at her with hooded, unreadable eyes. A muscle drummed in the hard line of his jaw, his full lips slightly parted. The tip of his tongue caressed his bottom lip, leaving a wet trail, the Adam's apple in his thick throat bobbing as he swallowed. Jocelyn stilled. It wasn't a stretch to let her mind envision that tongue leaving a similar glistening path on her skin...or what those lips would feel like licking and sucking their way down her body. Her nipples drew tight with need, breath catching in her lungs.

She cleared a dry throat. "I suppose none of this is new to you."

"Watching *you* watch is new to me."

"I'm not a prude," she said.

"Never said you were." His eyes flicked to the woman who had arched her back and was moaning when her attendants replaced their hands with their mouths. "Does this excite you?"

Jocelyn exhaled. "Yes."

"Being with multiple partners?" he prodded.

She shook her head—she couldn't even imagine being with one, much less four, though the *idea* of it was scintillating. All that sensation had to be overwhelming. She was only observing, and already her body felt coiled and ready to burst at the barest promise of touch.

"Being so exposed," she replied. "Does the lady not care that people are watching?" They weren't the only ones standing near the glass observing the show.

"She enjoys it," Westmore said. "To her, it's a performance. Sometimes it's a man in the place of the woman, surrounded by whoever brings him pleasure. We don't discriminate."

Jocelyn frowned. "Is she an actress?"

"A posture moll."

"What is that?"

The duke shrugged. "A performer of sorts. She poses, dances or does other things for entertainment. Anything she pleases, really.

London isn't called the *wicked city* for nothing." He waved an arm. "In here, anything is permitted, as long as all parties agree. Our single golden rule, as you know by now." Westmore called over a gorgeous footman, and Jocelyn felt her cheeks warm at the man's shirtless gold-dusted muscles. "Drink?"

The duke was watching her when he handed her the glass filled with champagne. Only it wasn't an ordinary glass. No, this one was hand-blown into the curvaceous shape of a woman's breast, complete with shaded areola and distended nipple with a hole through it meant for sipping. Jocelyn sucked in a breath, hiding her appalled reaction. "Are you trying to shock me, Your Grace?"

"If I meant to shock you, my lady, I would have offered you this one." He smiled. "Though, in hindsight, you *did* demand it upstairs."

This time, she choked on her own spit. The one he held was blown in the shape of a man's sexual organ. Thank God it was dark because her cheeks felt like they were on fire, and down below, her core clenched on air. Over a sodding glass. "Lovely, though whoever the model must have been overcompensating for something. That thing is enormous."

A wicked smile crossed his face, making a shiver race through her. "I suppose you'll have to see for yourself."

"*You* were the model?" She gaped at him, eyes dashing back to the vessel, her tongue coming out to wet her dry lips.

"A gentleman never tells."

"If you are indeed telling the truth, isn't it a bit vainglorious to be drinking from a glass made in the mold of one's own genitals?"

"Perfection should be celebrated at all times," he replied succinctly.

Jocelyn couldn't help it, she laughed. She had never expected to experience this side of a man who was rumored to be fractious and cold, and ruthless in business, not this playful, charming version who didn't seem to take himself too seriously or who drank from a cock-shaped glass with aplomb. Which was the real version of him, she wondered. She'd be naïve to think the hard-nosed brutal duke wasn't in there somewhere.

He was not known as the Wolf of Westmore for nothing.

She needed the reminder that the more time she spent with him, *conversing* with him, the faster she would expose herself. Time was of the essence. Exhaling, Jocelyn turned to face him and ran one finger down his sleeve. "Are there private rooms down here?"

Hooded, gleaming eyes met hers. "Yes."

"Show me."

CHAPTER 4

Pouring himself some expensive Scotch whisky from the stocked mantel in a plain tumbler, Wulfric watched her through a heavy-lidded gaze as she prowled the perimeter of the private apartments. He still could not shake the feeling that he recognized her from somewhere. But he met dozens of ladies in any given month at The Silver Scythe, not to mention the female aristocrats in London ballrooms. His lovely mistress of the hour could be anyone.

"Whisky?" he asked her.

She gave a short, decisive shake of her head, and then pinned her lips, changing the gesture to a nod. "Some sherry, if you have it."

"We do." He poured a glass, a much less obscene one this time, and handed it to her.

She arched a brow, several shades lighter than her dark hair. "No prick glass?"

His prick jumped as if it'd been personally addressed. "Alas, that's only in the main room.

We're much more sedate in our dish choices behind closed doors."

That red mouth curled in a smile so sinful that he felt it in his ballocks. "Pity."

Wulfric had to admit that she'd taken the vulgar glasses in stride. Perhaps he'd been wrong in his estimation of her as well. Wouldn't be the first time. He'd had the sneaking suspicion for some time that Roth's own marchioness was the infamous Lady Darcy, author of the scandalous sex periodical, not that he would share that with his best friend, but Lady Roth was one of those women who had many, *many* secret layers. Perhaps this Lady J was the same.

A tempest behind a veneer of elegance.

"What makes this different to other bawdy clubs in London?" his guest asked, her steps taking her near to the enormous bed with its decadent wine-colored silk counterpane and frilled pillows. Once a room had been enjoyed, servants were very efficient in their duties, the entire space cleaned from top to bottom. It amounted to a mountain of laundry, but supplied jobs to those who wanted honest work... paid for by the very deep pockets of the members who kept them in business.

A win-win.

Her question took him by surprise because it was underscored by what sounded like true interest, not an attempt at small conversation. "It's not a brothel, my lady." When a skeptical gleam came into her expression with a pointed glance at the bed, he spread his hands wide. "Call it a social club with a twist. We cater to an exclusive, elegant clientele, and we're in the business of pleasure. Excellent food, games and revelry, and if that extends to a bedchamber or three, so be it. Our staff is free of disease, our spaces private and clean, and our patrons can enjoy themselves in any way they want, free of censure, judgment, and punishment. Life should be indulged, shouldn't it?"

"Isn't all this against the law?"

"Whose law? The church? The crown? Parliament? Men or women are their own governance when it comes to their own bodies. We might be the epitome of the civilized world in drawing rooms, at White's, or the Royal Opera, but here within these very private walls, you can choose to drink, smoke, consume, gamble, dance, watch, fuck."

She gasped at the last, her body giving a delicious sort of shiver, eyelashes dipping down to hide her reaction. Deep color distilled down the slim column of her throat to her collarbones, like ink through water. She was aroused—it was obvious in that telltale flush over her pretty skin, the shallowness of her breaths, and the constant way her tongue flicked out to wet her lips. God, she was lovely.

Who was she?

Why does it matter?

It didn't matter. It shouldn't matter, but the mystery was begging to be solved. Not to mention his cock was more eager than it had been in some time. As much as he played the rake in his position at the club, he preferred a quiet evening spent with his estate ledgers and a good Scottish whisky than the debauchery he was reputed for. He and Roth had shared a similar reputation for years. They were known as libertines of the first water, and people believed what they wanted to believe. In truth, Wulfric hadn't been with a woman in years.

Not since Prue's death.

Seeing her in that filthy opium den had cut something from him...any ability to feel had died with her that day. Oh, he continued to play the part of the dissolute rake that was expected of him, but it was all a performance.

"And what of adultery?" Lady J asked. "Men and women who break their vows?"

"Their decisions are on them." He gave a careless shrug. "And how do *you* know what goes on behind closed doors? We have many married couples who come here together, seeking adventure or to share mutual fantasies in a safe space. One can easily judge when one is on a high horse."

She snorted. "I assure you, Your Grace, if there is a steed involved, I'm being dragged behind it like chattel, not sitting atop it."

Cocking his head, Wulfric stared at her, his opinions shifting yet again. What did *that* mean? Was she a widow? A scorned wife? Or had he been wrong about her being a peeress and she was simply a high-class courtesan thrown aside by her lord and protector for a younger one? He couldn't countenance that—

who would discard such a prize? The skin of her cheeks was smooth, the porcelain skin youthful. Her lips...his eyes fastened on that lush bow, painted in the same hue of her garments, and he felt his length stiffen more when he imagined that perfect pout leaving red smudges upon him.

Turning toward the adjoining antechamber, he discreetly adjusted himself and leaned against the wall, watching her finish the rest of her wandering exploration. He frowned, the possibilities narrowing, but still endless. Perhaps she was a fallen lady, a *former* aristocrat, who had been compromised in some way. Or better yet, an unmarried heiress out to make mischief. He snorted a laugh at that—sheltered misses would faster swoon before setting foot here.

Eventually, she stopped to perch on a gold-covered armchair, the scarlet folds of her cloak billowing about her.

"What do you do with the money?" she asked. "From the auction?" She wet her lips again and folded her hands in her lap. "Do you keep any of it?"

"No, all the proceeds are donated to charity. A women's shelter."

"That's commendable," she murmured.

Wulfric didn't know why the next words came out of his mouth. Maybe it was the dubious way she said it, as if she didn't quite believe they would send every penny made from an outrageous auction at an equally outrageous club to such a place. "I knew a girl once who needed help and didn't get it. She died. The charity is in her name."

A wide green stare collided with his. Her hands, so expressive, lifted from her lap to tug at a button on her cloak, a look of distress coming over her face that she tried to smooth away with a trembling smile. A muscle worked in her throat. Had she lost someone too? Not for the first time, Wulfric wished he could see the entirety of her face.

Oddly, the small thread of commonality between them meant something, even if she was a stranger he'd never see again. Wulfric downed the glass of whisky, relishing the burn...and the forced clarity it brought. It didn't matter who she was, only what she'd contributed. Setting down his tumbler, he cleared his throat. "What do you wish of me?"

More color suffused her skin before that chin of hers jutted upward, a sure sign that she was reaching for internal fortification. "Could you..." She let out a hiss of breath through her teeth and fisted her fingers in her skirts. "May I see what my charitable donation has bought me?"

"You want me to undress?"

A roll of that lower lip beneath the upper. "If you will."

Slowly, Wulfric shrugged out of his coat, and then his waistcoat. All the while, he felt her stare intent upon him, the shallow, quick rises of her chest, the only indication she was breathing. When he tugged his shirt over his head, leaving his upper body bare and on display, he met her gaze boldly. That bottom lip of hers was wedged between her teeth, posture rigid as if she didn't trust herself quite yet to relax.

"Shall I continue?" he asked.

"Yes," she replied hoarsely. "The rest, please."

If it wasn't for the slight quiver in her voice, Wulfric would have believed the convincing show of sangfroid. He sat on the bench at the end of the bed and removed his boots and stockings, until he was only clad in his trousers.

"You're not finished," she pointed out.

"The rest is for you to unwrap," he drawled, primal satisfaction building in him at the hiss of indrawn breath when that gaze fell to the obnoxious bulge at his groin that he made no move to hide.

He prowled toward her, stopping only when he was nearly on top of her. He leaned down and propped his hands on either side of the arm rests, caging her small body in. The pulse at her throat fluttered like a captive, panicked thing, but she met his look without hesitation.

"Don't be afraid," he whispered, bending even more to feather his mouth along one side of her temple before pulling back to do the same on the other side. She smelled of crushed lilacs.

"I am not."

That was true, he realized with delayed astonishment. In the spare candlelight, the green looked like molten jade, flecks of gold visible in their heated depths. She might have been nervous and excited, but there was no fear in that

wide gaze. No, in her stare, he saw drive and resolve, and enough desire to match the tide
teeming through his blood. Still watching him,
she removed her gloves, exposing smooth skin
and long elegant fingers.

Definitely the hands of a lady.

Surprising him, she slowly pushed her body
upward, making him straighten, even as her
breasts grazed his torso and chest. Wulfric
found himself being the one to inhale, his lungs
going tight when her sweet flowery fragrance
wafted into his nostrils. *Fuuuuuck.* He had experienced physical attraction with women in the
past, but nothing had ever quite been this siz-
zling. This raw. The level of arousal felt like he
was going to peel out of his own skin, his cock
so fucking hard, it hurt to even breathe.

And that was *before* her fingers went to the
ties of that cloak, *before* they released the fastenings, and *before* the fabric descended into a
scarlet pool at her heels, taking every god-
damned ounce of his good sense with it. Because the bloody chit was wearing nothing but a
tiny pair of cream-colored short stays, embroidered with pink flowers, over the filmiest
chemise known to man.

Hell if she wasn't every erotic fantasy come
to life.

Wulfric's throat went unspeakably dry while
his cock tried to punch a hole in the fabric of his
trousers. He didn't know where to look...at the
lush expanse of her breasts, the curves of her
small waist and generous hips flaring beneath

the embroidered sateen panels of her stays, the long lines of her legs and the shadowed apex of her thighs just visible through the sheer lawn.

"Like what you see?" she whispered, lifting her face to his dazed one.

"You're bloody stunning."

Blushing, she smiled and twined her arms around his nape. "I am here for your pleasure, Your Grace. And mine, of course."

CHAPTER 5

W here she found such boldness, Jocelyn would never know.

Inside, her body felt like a mass of jelly. Because, *heavens*, the sight of that man unclothed had turned every bone, every muscle, and every brain cell to complete mush. Had anyone ever been built so perfectly? So godlike in his masculine beauty?

The duke was not stocky, but he was tall and obviously strong. Shelves upon shelves of sleek, golden muscle, from his wiry shoulders to the deeply grooved abdomen to those ropy, veiny forearms dusted in dark hair, had made it utterly impossible to breathe. To move.

To *think*!

Because here was the Wolf of Westmore in all his predatory glory.

Those orange-hued eyes of his glowed, his black pupils huge, like a lunar eclipse with a darkened sun gilding its edges. His jaw was hard, full lips pulled taut. And his scent... God, she could bask in it. Rub herself in that warm leather-and-bergamot aroma like a shameless vixen in heat. Jocelyn bit back a snort. She'd be his lady wolf any day.

The space between her legs practically *throbbed* with want. She could feel her heartbeat echoing there like a drum, announcing to all and sundry that the enormous vessel in his pants was more than welcome into her empty harbor. Jocelyn nearly snorted again at the absurd metaphor, and then swallowed her mirth, as a pulse of anxiety surged. Her body felt wet and ready, but she'd never done this before. Would it hurt? Should she say anything? What if she bled?

No, no, no. Gentlemen did not like hearing such things…it would cause him to stop and question.

And she didn't want questions. She wanted action.

If there was blood, at least the dark red sheets would hide it. One of her older sisters had bled, though the other hadn't, and their experiences in the bedchamber had been wildly different. Jocelyn blinked rapidly, heart racing with excitement and panic. Excitement for what was to come, and panic that her greenness would be immediately apparent to a proficient lover like Westmore. Dear God, would he see right through her?

"I haven't done this many times," she admitted in a low whisper.

There, that would do.

"I'll be gentle." A palm banded around her back as another arm reached under her legs.

In the next breath, she was swooped up into his sinewy arms and ferried over to the bed. The mattress at her back was soft, not that she expected lumps since everything about The Silver Scythe was designed for luxury and comfort. Why would a bordello bed be any different?

Good gracious, are you really doing this?

Closing her eyes, Jocelyn shook away the prim voice in her head. If her parents wanted to sell her to the Marquess of Perrin, she would damn well be sure he didn't get everything. This was for her, and so what if she had paid for the pleasure? Every penny went to charity. Heavens, she'd almost broken down when he'd confessed whom the shelter was for. She knew...Jocelyn *knew* it was for Prudence. It'd been no secret that the Duke of Westmore had loved Prue deeply.

A secret charity in her name was just like him.

Jocelyn bit her lip and tried to bring herself back to the moment—this chamber was no place for parents or the ghosts of dead friends. This chamber was for *her*, for the man about to receive the gift her body could only offer once, and for shared gratification.

She wrinkled her nose. She *hoped* it would be gratifying. She'd been an avid reader of the Lady Darcy periodicals, which touted that pleasure was to be had for both men and women during sexual congress. It was thanks to that racy publication that she had felt confident enough in her own power as a female to go after what she wanted. Specifically, the Duke of Westmore. At least, before she was bartered to a gout-ridden fossil for a parcel of land and a title.

"Where did you go just then?" the duke asked, watching her.

Jocelyn's eyes flicked open behind her mask. "Nowhere. I'm right here."

"Good girl." Those feral orange-lit eyes glittered with dominance, making her insides promptly turn to jelly again. Then he kissed her, his hard male lips taking hers in a kiss so tender her toes curled. Per the periodical, his tongue would come next. There *was* a thing as too much tongue, Lady Darcy had cautioned, and Jocelyn braced for entry, but all she felt was firm, soft pressure, followed by a sinful, velvet swipe over her bottom lip. She tasted whisky and a dark flavor that was all him, and she wanted more.

Playfully, he nibbled at her lips, drawing his tongue—*definitely not too much*—along the seam of her mouth before she opened for him in invitation. He swept in, a silken invasion as his tongue teased hers, coaxing it into his own mouth. She went greedily and was rewarded when he groaned and kissed her deeper, stealing the breath from her lungs.

"You do that well," she gasped, when he pulled away.

His eyes hooded. "So do you."

Delighted, she pressed her tingling lips together. If only he knew that Lady Darcy recommended practicing with one's hand curled into a loose fist, with the thumb and upper curve of the forefinger mimicking a pair of lips, as well as with a ripe apricot, he might be shocked. She couldn't believe the technique had actually worked.

All hail Lady Darcy, the devoted champion of female pleasure!

According to the publication, there was more to come, including kisses elsewhere. As in down *there*. That indecent throb at her core began anew. Would a man truly do such a thing? Kiss a lady between her thighs? Would Westmore? She had washed in lilac-scented water, even taken a pair of scissors to her maidenhair —grooming was more of a courtesan thing according to Lady Darcy—but she'd wanted to be perfect.

Jocelyn froze. Oh, *hell*. Her maidenhair!

She'd worn a dark wig, her wealth of red hair much too noticeable. Would the duke notice the difference? Remark upon it? And even more importantly, *could* a man recognize a woman by something like that? As much as she longed to discover whether the duke was proficient in the artistry of the tongue, per Lady Darcy, she could not risk it.

One warm hand slid up her leg, making her shiver and forget her momentary worry. When his mouth traveled to her neck, Jocelyn tried to relax, but her whole body felt as though it was on fire. His other hand was not idle as he unlaced the tie at the top of her chemise and stays, and nuzzled between her breasts.

"Do you like breast play?" he asked, his voice like gravel.

"I…" *Don't know.* Jocelyn clamped her lips together, just as his fingers brushed her nipple and her spine bowed.

"I'll take that as a yes." When his mouth dipped to take the aching peak into his mouth, Jocelyn's eyes nearly rolled back into her head as lightning tore through her entire body. His tongue swirled, his teeth scraped, and she writhed. By the time he moved down to remove her shoes and roll down her stockings, she was delirious with need. He bit at her knee, licked up the inside of her thigh and spread them wide. When she glanced down at the wanton picture his broad shoulders pushing her knees apart made, she trembled.

"I can't wait to taste you," he growled, nostril flaring as though he was ready to pounce.

Yes, for the love of all things wicked, yes!

Wait, no! Positively no.

"No, please stop," she said, reaching down to keep the hem of chemise over her groin. "I'm shy."

His eyes widened, even as a sultry smirk tugged the corner of his full lips upward. "Is that a fact?"

"Yes," she said on a ragged breath. Damn her disguise to purgatory!

"Fingers?" he asked.

She nodded mutely, that heated, hungry stare

too much to take. He didn't look upset at her refusal, only a speculative gleam appearing for a moment before it disappeared. Perhaps he'd chalk it down to her inexperience. Pushing up onto those lean forearms, he crawled up her body and she felt the bare heat of his hair-roughened legs against her skin. When had he discarded his trousers? It was on the tip of her tongue to demand her unwrapping rights, when two fingers slid through the copious amounts of wetness at the juncture of her thighs.

"Guh…"

"You're drenched," he said, lifting his fingers between them, glossed in the shine of her essence. Without releasing her gaze, he slid them into his mouth, a low groan of pleasure rumbling from him. Jocelyn stared in shock as he sucked them clean. "As I thought, delicious. Nothing at all to be shy about, I promise you."

The dark, indelicate rasp nearly made her shove him back down there and tell him to go to work, discovery be damned. "You're very wicked, Your Grace," she said.

"Wickedness is a matter of perspective, my lady." He lapped at her tight nipple and took it between his teeth, biting just hard enough for her to feel the edge of pain, before soothing it with his efficient tongue. She moaned as heat rushed into the smarting peak. "I could dine on you for hours, lick every crevice of this beautiful body." His palm reached behind to squeeze a full handful of her behind. "See *my* marks on this creamy skin."

Her brain went blank.

"You would spank me?" Her voice was so breathy she barely recognized it, even as her heartrate tripled behind her ribs as the image of the couple from the windowed room flashed into her brain. The man had seemed in raptures.

"Do you want me to?"

Did she? Biting her lip as her body scorched and burned, she gave one nod.

With barely any warning, he lifted them both up, sat himself on the edge of the bed and splayed her over his bent knees. Jocelyn could feel his hardened erection prodding into her stomach that was still guarded by the fabric of her stays. Cool air kissed her bottom, when he lifted the hem of her chemise over her cheeks.

"What a lovely canvas," he said, running a hand over her skin in a small circle.

He gave no warning other than the absence of his touch, the flat of his palm connecting with the fleshiest part of her. She gasped. The initial shock of it was worse than any actual pain. Three successive strikes followed to alternating sides, and her body tightened at each one. It hurt, as she'd expected it would. Jocelyn frowned. Where was the pleasure? Why had that man looked delirious with it, when his partner had been using a whip?

She opened her mouth about to tell him to stop, that this wasn't for her, when he completed two more, one on each cheek, followed by a soothing rub that ended with his fingers dipping between her legs. Two fingers grazed over the heart of her. Suddenly the heat spreading across her bottom from the strikes blended into warmth she felt everywhere. In her nipples, in her cheeks—upper and lower—and in her sex.

Jocelyn gasped when those probing fingers delved into her saturated core, a pleased rumble breaking from him at what he found. The amount of moisture leaking from her had to be indecent, and the vulgar sounds her body made around his fingers were mortifying, though shame was the least of the emotions barreling through her. Her core was tight and so hot, every part of her sex alive with sensation.

She almost cried when he withdrew, her body clenching on air. Jocelyn was so wound up, she knew it wouldn't take much to send her hurtling over the edge, and when two more strikes rained down on her overheated, tender flesh, she bit into the bedclothes, her body so strained it felt as though she was going to explode out of her skin.

"Westmore," she begged, back arched helplessly up. "I can't."

"You can." A pair of successive strikes on each side and her bottom was officially on fire. *Everything* was on fire, but those flames were tempered in honeyed bliss.

Thick fingers sank into her passage again, scissoring slightly once or twice, then pulled out to graze lightly over the tight bundle of nerves at the top of her sex, and Jocelyn's back bowed with the force of her release. Ecstasy pounded through her in waves, her vision going white as her body convulsed around Westmore's fingers. She screamed into the bedclothes as her body detonated like a lit fuse, blowing every part of her into sublime rapture.

As she drifted, riding the waves of pleasure, he brought her upright with one arm, cradling her limp upper body to his chest, and took her lips with his in a drugging kiss. "You're so responsive," he told her while planting heated kisses to her jaw and her neck as he rolled her to her back and positioned himself between her legs. "So fucking beautiful when you come." Jocelyn could barely function, her mind lost in the aftermath of her orgasm. "You'll do it again, all over my cock."

Yes, please, Duke...

When he pushed carefully and slowly inside her, it was thanks to his extensive preparation that Jocelyn felt nothing but an intense kind of fullness. He wasn't done, her dull brain realized, as he eased gently backward only to push in further. It stung as he stretched her. *Oh,* that was a lot. She tensed around him with a frown, and he stilled. "Are you well?"

"You're big," she said with a breathless moan. The edge of pain was riding the edge of pleasure, and she needed the pleasure to take over. He was too large, his body pressing her and her sore bottom into the sheets. "And my behind stings."

Westmore chuckled. "I'll rub some salve in it after, I promise."

"Make me feel good again, Your Grace."

"Wulfric," he said, staring down at her, right before sliding his fingers to where they were joined, his thumb unerringly finding the needy spot that made her gasp and ripple around him. "That's it," he said, circling the area, while easing backward and stroking in, filling her more each time.

Pleasure coiled in languid ropes when his mouth latched on to her neck, nibbling up to her earlobe, before claiming her mouth in a kiss so fierce, all she could feel was him working her body at both ends...making her his. When he was fully seated, and so deep she didn't know where either of them began or ended, Westmore—no, Wulfric—started to move.

One powerful thrust, and dear Lord, if her body didn't seize and explode then and there.

"Wulfric!" she whimpered, stars bursting behind her eyes.

Jocelyn could only hold on as her second release catapulted her into space, her fingers digging into the tight meat of his shoulders as that strong body drilled into her, chasing his pleasure on the heels of hers. All she knew was that if she let go of him, she'd be torn away on the surge of pleasure taking her body in its unyielding grip.

But more than ever, all Jocelyn wanted to do was watch him. That handsome face was tight with strain, lips parted and eyes burning with lust. She'd never seen anything more incredible in her life than this man poised at the pinnacle of his passion. A formidable wolf between her legs. *Her* wolf…at least in this moment.

Powerful, magnificent, wild.

With a growl torn from the depths of him, that long, sinewy body stilled for one glorious moment, head thrown back and corded veins pulsing at his neck, he withdrew from her still quivering body to spend in the sheets between them. When he collapsed with a groan and took them both to their sides, Jocelyn had no words for what she'd just experienced.

She didn't care about Perrin. She didn't care about her parents. She didn't care about anything but the fact that she was wholly, divinely, *deliciously* replete.

CHAPTER 6

Wulfric pinched the bridge of his nose with his thumb and forefinger, and leaned back in his chair, the beginnings of a headache gnawing at the edges of his skull. The desk was covered with a mountain of papers. Normally, he loved poring over his estate accounts, financial investments, and making money hand over fist. Columns of numbers made sense to him, calmed him, but today he was distracted. The last *week* he'd been distracted.

All he could think about was a dark-haired minx who had invaded his mind.

Who was she?

After what had to be one of the most satisfying sexual encounters of his life, the woman he'd bedded had risen, presumably retied the fastenings of that voluminous cloak over nothing at all, and taken her leave. While he had been asleep…and all without saying one word.

Wulfric put his head in his hands and groaned. Sex of that nature was supposed to be detached. He shouldn't care for anything but how good it had been and leave the interlude where it belonged, but for the life of him, he couldn't stop thinking about her.

Obsessing about her.

Not to mention that he was the butt of all kind of jokes, ever since he'd bolted up from that empty bed and darted out into the foyer in nothing but a cushion to cover his half-masted cock, whereupon he had come face-to-face with none other than the Marquess of Roth, who had stared at him and lifted a brow in flagrant amusement.

"Do I even want to know?" he'd asked.

"Dark hair, red mask, red cloak. Did you see her?"

"Lady J, I presume?" Roth had asked and Wulfric had nodded. "No, I had my own female problems to contend with in the form of my willful wife. Did you find out who your mistress of the evening was?"

"No."

That brow had arched higher. "Will you?"

"She's gone, so no."

"Losing your touch, Westmore?" Roth had taunted. "Normally they're back here begging for seconds and thirds."

"You damn well know that was before..." He'd trailed off as a look of stark pain had come over Roth's face. He hadn't even had to finish the sentence. *Before Prue.* They both had their demons when it came to his sister.

Without waiting for a reply, Wulfric had stalked back into the chamber that had still smelled of crushed lilacs, irrationally angry. He'd wanted to sit in that room and breathe in the last of her. He'd also wanted to tear it apart so he could banish it from memory. In the end, he had dressed quietly, like a civilized man, and left to see to his many pressing ducal duties.

But honestly, what kind of woman ran out on a man?

The kind that didn't want to be identified, his brain supplied. He shouldn't be surprised. The Silver Scythe dealt in secrets, thousands of them. What was one more, with skin so soft, he stiffened thinking about that reddened arse and the copious amounts of arousal between those slender legs. What about her entranced him so?

Beyond the incredible physical connection, that was.

Wulfric snorted. He couldn't remember ever in his life spending so hard that his brain had blanked, and thank God, he'd had the where-withal to withdraw. Normally, that was the sole thing on his mind—complete mastery over his body, to the end that he was used to finishing himself off in hand, just to be safe—but this time, he'd been so lost that he'd pulled out at the last possible moment. A half-second more, and he might have had a lot more to contend with than not knowing who she was.

And yet, even that thought wasn't as appalling as it should have been.

"Pull yourself together, damn it," he muttered, and then cursed as ink splattered over his fingers. He cursed even harder when he realized that he'd doodled the letter J in the margins of his ledgers like a besotted finishing-school miss.

"Begging your pardon, Your Grace!" His normally efficient butler knocked, looking like his hair was standing on end.

"What is it, Hall?"

"The Marquess of Roth sent a note with an address in Covent Garden. There's trouble. The marquess's brother, Lord Oliver, is here and he's got Runners with him."

Worried that it might be trouble at the women's shelter, Wulfric didn't stop to think, he bolted to his feet. "Coat, hat, carriage."

"Already waiting, Your Grace."

"Good man."

Within short order, he was on his way to Seven Dials on the heels of Oliver, Roth's brother. What the devil had Roth gotten himself into now? Wulfric was in a state of dread, because the address on the note was right near Prue's shelter house. Were any of the women there in danger?

But when the carriage came to a stop, all he could see was Roth and his marchioness glaring at each other. The altercation, perhaps a mugging gone wrong, seemed to be over. The Runners were quick to take an irate but injured man—whom Wulfric belatedly recognized as the disgraced, former Earl of Beaumont, Edmund Cain—into custody, and the situation looked to be in hand, until it wasn't. Cain pulled a gun from nowhere and pointed at Roth's wife. "Shoot me, and she dies, too," he shouted.

Wulfric froze where he stood. Everyone did. "Put down the gun, Cain," he called out. "Even if you get the shot off, we both know what will happen." Cain mumbled something to Roth, and Wulfric saw his hand tighten on the weapon. "Don't try it!"

But it was too late. The sound of a gunshot renting the air made him jerk into action, but two men went down as Oliver crashed into his brother. By the time the Runners had restrained Cain, Wulfric was across the square to assess the damage. Oliver had taken the shot meant for the marchioness, while Roth had had the same idea to leap in front of his wife. Thankfully, Roth had only a shallow gash on his head, and they would both survive.

Something ached in Wulfric's chest as he watched his best friend and his wife hold each other, their every emotion transparent. Suddenly, he wanted that. He wanted someone to give a shit whether he was dead or alive. An image of clear green eyes danced over his vision, and he shoved it away. *She* was no one to him. Nothing but a passing piece of muslin, and it was better that way.

And besides, he had other things to deal with before any thought of marriage.

Destroying the Duke of Tyne was paramount.

∾

JOCELYN'S EYES scanned her book as she munched on a half-eaten apple. She was pretending to read, but was straining her ears and avidly listening to the conversation between her papa and her cousin Tybalt, her father's heir, at the other end of the library. They had not seen her in her quiet, favorite little nook. Something about an attack on the Marquess of Roth and his wife in Covent Garden by some shoddy earl, over a fortnight past. Along with everyone in London, she'd heard the gossip, of course, of the despicable earl who had pursued both the Duchess of Beswick as well as her younger sister, the Marchioness of Roth, almost to ruin.

Jocelyn bit her lip. She was in a similar boat, about to be traded to a marriage prospect like the bartering tool she was. Unfortunately, unlike Isobel Everleigh, she did not have any intrepid older sisters looking out for her, or in the case of her elder sister Astrid, a powerful duke who'd wage wars for her. Exhaling, her thoughts drifted to Westmore, and she banished them as quickly as they'd come. If the duke truly knew who she was, he'd use her for the sport of it, probably to get at her father. No, it was better that he never knew.

"It says that devil Westmore was there as well," Tybalt said, drawing her instant attention.

Her body jerked with alarm. Had the duke been hurt? "Too bad he didn't get shot," her cousin went on in a vicious tone.

"That would have solved our problems," her father agreed. "It should be our good fortune that one day, some brave soul will call him out. For the honor of the Capehart name."

Jocelyn stiffened—was her father insinuating that *Tybalt* should call the duke out? She hoped her cousin wasn't that stupid. Her father hated Westmore with an unhealthy passion, but premeditated murder was a step too far.

The Duke of Westmore had made no secret of undermining any investment her father showed interest in—steamships, locomotive expansion, mining or manufacturing contracts, anything at all—he went over and above to snatch it from beneath her papa's nose. It drove her father mad, Jocelyn knew, but the bitter feud between their families had been ongoing for centuries. Stolen lands, stolen brides, stolen property. Back and forth like children bickering over toys. Jocelyn was sick of it.

It was the sole reason she was being married off to Perrin.

For land on the eastern coast, and an estate that included a portion of valuable shoreline. Her father had crowed that Westmore would have to marry Perrin himself to thwart the plans for enlargement of their family's shipping ports. Jocelyn sighed. There was to be a masked ball in a week for the purpose of introductions. Introductions, her eyeball! The betrothal agreement had practically already been inked and put to dry. The thought of being salivated over and touched by the old lecher made her feel ill.

Could she somehow escape the ball? Feign sickness? Feign *death*?

Come now, you're being melodramatic, Jocelyn! You're a clever girl, you'll think of something. Death is no answer to one's troubles.

But her usually wily mind came up blank. Her fate was sealed. Short of running away with the rest of her jewels, which wouldn't last more than a year, if that, since she'd sold most of them to pay for her evening of passionate ruination.

Jocelyn wrapped her arms about herself and took comfort in that. At least, she had the memory of what had been the best night of her life. Could *that* sustain her when the Marquess of Perrin heaved his old, gout-ridden body to rut into hers?

She shuddered. How did so many ladies put up with such marriages?

Lie there and think of England.

She'd rather eat gruel for the rest of her life. Jocelyn had no doubt she'd find a way to avoid her future husband somehow. And perhaps she might be lucky. Men his age died suddenly all the time. Perhaps fate would be kind and the marquess would drop dead in the next few weeks, right before the ball at which her father intended to announce their betrothal. And, well, if he didn't die, then she would simply have to make the best of it.

Lie back and think of every country in the world.

In alphabetical order.

Perhaps her costume for the masque should be an old crone covered in warts. Maybe if she disgusted him enough, Perrin might change his mind. Jocelyn giggled at the image of herself in the ugliest disguise she could muster. Her father would never allow it and would punish her severely, but heavens, the idea of it tickled her to no end. After her wedding vows, she would make herself so disagreeable that her husband would wince to come near her.

With that energizing thought, she closed her book and headed back to her chamber. Perhaps she'd go for a ride to curb the restlessness in her blood. It was the only thing she could do that tired her out enough so she stopped trying to find Westmore at every party she attended. Tonight was a ball at the Duchess of Beswick's and she knew he would not be there. The man simply did not do *ton* events.

Was he at The Silver Scythe? With other women? The thought wracked her. A man like him would not be without female company. He was too virile, too handsome, too *everything*.

One evening a week ago, she'd had to stop herself from sneaking off to the West End, just to see if she could catch a glimpse of him at the address she'd memorized from the invitation, but she wasn't a member and would not be allowed entry. Besides, there was the risk of exposure. Then she'd heard a few days later, via Tybalt's ranting, that Westmore was in the country with the Marquess of Roth in Chelmsford. That had cooled her heels somewhat.

Until of course, her mind had wondered if he'd been in Chelmsford for one of Roth's raunchy country parties with its equally raunchy guests, which had sent her off on yet another horseback ride to calm her emotions... and her hopeless jealousy.

Why the devil couldn't she stop fantasizing about him?

CHAPTER 7

Wulfric adjusted his mask—a snarling wolf. Fitting for the occasion, since he was infiltrating enemy territory. His man of business had reported that Tyne was on the cusp of obtaining access to a tract of coastland that would fatten his coffers. Wulfric frowned. The land in question was entailed, which meant that Tyne, that devious bastard, was going to marry his last remaining daughter off to get it.

He vaguely remembered being introduced to Lady Jocelyn Capehart, Prue's best friend from finishing school. A petite, demure, redheaded chit, if he recalled. Perrin would destroy her. But it wasn't his concern whether an old man debauched an innocent girl. He needed to figure out how to stop Tyne from getting what he wanted, and short of finding a replacement bride or an offer that would turn Perrin's loyalty, he was out of ideas.

Wulfric prowled the perimeter of the ballroom, and then his heart jumped, caught by a figure at the top of the stairs. A brunette in red. His breath hitched, every part of him going on high alert, before disappointment was quick to set in. It wasn't her.

He almost laughed at himself. Lady J would not be *here*.

Chances were that his lover wasn't even one of the aristocracy at all, at least not one to be invited to Tyne's affair. The man only associated with the *crème de la crème* of the *ton*. Not that Wulfric had been invited—he'd finagled his way in through a side entrance. Tyne would have conniptions if he knew his sworn enemy was in his house.

At least, he was sure Lady J hadn't been a courtesan, or at least an experienced one. One, no courtesan worth her salt would give up two-and-a-half thousand quid for charity. Two, her lack of proficiency had been obvious, though somewhere deep down, that had pleased him. Wulfric liked knowing she hadn't had many lovers before him. He hoped, whoever she was, that he'd ruined her for any other man. That she thought about him as often as he thought about her. Which was every hour of every damned day. He chuckled to himself.

If she hadn't left, would *he* have crept off in silence, as he usually did?

She'd beaten him to it, the minx.

Scanning the crowd, his eyes snagged on a young woman in a bright gold gown, a scarlet sash beneath her breasts as she danced with the

Duke of Tyne. He could not see her face, but a head of shining red curls, twined through with diamonds and pearls, made him stare for a protracted moment. Christ, what was his preoccupation with that color? Everywhere he went, he found himself bludgeoned by it...as if red had suddenly become his nemesis.

More like his *weakness*.

His gaze settled on the couple, revulsion curling his stomach at the man who had sent his father to his death. Tyne might not have held the pistol, but he was responsible all the same for spreading the rumors of infidelity and bastard children that had sent his mother to Bedlam and his adulterous father to a cruel, if undeserved, fate.

Wulfric would not rest until Tyne had paid his pound of flesh.

You could ruin the daughter.

The thought slid into his head like silk, but he discarded it. His vengeance would be exacted on Tyne alone, not via underhanded means that would destroy an innocent girl. Wulfric had seen what Tyne's machinations had done to his mother—exposing her husband's latest lover, a married peeress, pregnant with his child—and the scandal had shattered the dowager. He would not wish such heartbreak on anyone, not even for revenge.

Besides, Tyne's chit had her own problems.

Wulfric directed his attention to where the Duke of Tyne was now in conversation with the Marquess of Perrin. The old man kept darting looks over to the duke's daughter and licking his chops like a man standing before his last supper. If he hadn't also been looking at the girl, Wulfric would have missed the shudder of revulsion that she didn't bother to hide, just before slipping out of sight behind a column and disappearing.

Good for her. He'd want to escape such a fate as well. Squinting at the two gentlemen, Wulfric moved closer to where the duke was standing. If he could hear what they were saying, perhaps he could come up with an alternate plan to weaken Tyne.

He spotted an alcove a shadowed balcony just above where the men were standing. That would do. Wulfric wasn't familiar with Tyne's home, but there had to be a servants' staircase somewhere about. He kept an eye on the moving footmen, serving drinks and carrying trays, and followed them. Hustling up some narrow stairs just before the kitchen, he made his way down a carpeted corridor that was lit with a single sconce.

Heading to where he remembered seeing the small Juliet balcony—the fancy indoor over-hang, likely copied from Shakespeare's play of the same name, that served no purpose beyond ostentatious decoration. That was just like Tyne, to be so excessive. Who had inside balconies in their ballrooms? It was just pretentious. Wulfric pushed aside the curtain and eased his large frame into the narrow space.

Only to discover that he wasn't alone.

"Oh, my apologies," he said in surprise.

"Hush!" the crouching redhead in the gold gown scolded. The overpowering scent of rosewater hit him. "Get down before you're seen!" A furious flash of a gaze assessed him and then fell away as quickly as it had risen. A panicked sound escaped her lips—fear of discovery, perhaps?—but she remained silent, spine as stiff as a board in her stooped position.

Torn between backing away and doing what he'd come there to do, Wulfric ducked down beside Tyne's youngest daughter. "I do beg your pardon."

"What are you even doing up here?" she muttered. "This is the private family wing."

"What are *you* doing?" he countered in a low, matching tone.

"What does it look like?" she shot back. "Resting for a moment. And I live here, so this is allowed. *You're* not allowed."

"Shall I leave?" He made to stand, and an urgent hand, gloved in delicate white kidskin, pressed down on his arm, as the Duke of Tyne, who was right below them, looked upward with a frown on his face. The lady was surprisingly strong.

"Don't move," she commanded in a soft, imperious whisper. "For the love of God, I beg you."

"What are you really hiding from?" he asked.

She almost didn't answer, her fingers squeezing reflexively on his arm as if she'd forgotten it was there. "I'm to marry the man Tyne is talking to," she replied eventually.

"And you don't wish to?"

A suffocated laugh left her. "Who would?"

"I don't know," he whispered. "He's quite handsome from this angle."

"We can only see his hat."

Wulfric hid his smile. "Precisely."

~

WHO KNEW that the Duke of Westmore had a sense of humor outside the bedroom?

Jocelyn had known it was him the moment he'd squatted down beside her. That smell of warm leather and bergamot was reminder enough. Why on earth was he here? And did her father know? Did Tybalt know? Her cousin was a hothead at the best of times—he would likely call the man out in the middle of the ball, or something worse, and get himself killed or arrested in the process.

The snarling wolf mask—fitting, if a bit on the nose, though that might be only to her—covered most of the duke's face, and he was dressed in formal black evening wear like most of the men in the room. For her part, and to the displeasure of her father, Jocelyn had refused to wear a mask at all. Let him see the daughter he was bargaining away for the sake of his precious fortune. And besides everyone knew who she was, so she hadn't made much effort to hide behind a disguise either. As much as she'd wanted to embody a crone, being herself had made more of a statement.

She hadn't expected to run into her former lover, however!

Not that Westmore would recognize her. She *hoped*.

Her breath had faltered when she'd looked up to see him, only to dip her chin in horror. Luckily, she'd worn a scent Perrin loathed, because it reminded him of his late marchioness—a small act of defiance to be perverse, she supposed. And she wasn't wearing a dark wig. She'd have to keep her voice to a whisper and hide her eyes. She wasn't taking any chances there. While a part of her would have loved to see the look of shock on his face, Jocelyn would not be held responsible for him facing down her father or her cousin.

Her body had gone molten, however, in pure muscle memory, heat firing over all her nerve endings. Gracious, it wasn't normal to feel so unsettled by a man, was it? Her nipples turned to stone beneath her bodice, every inch of skin tightening, and her core clenching at the visceral memory of him. What would it be like to be his permanent lover? To be taken every which way known to man, each night? A pulse of rabid envy shot through her.

They had only coupled once, before she'd lost her nerve and left while he was sleeping, but Jocelyn knew there were many other erotic positions. The minute she'd returned home from her racy adventure, she scoured her collection of Lady Darcy periodicals for any information she could find on the subject.

According to the knowledgeable old biddy, there was quite a bit. A woman could ride a man. He could take her from behind—*that* particular designation had left her breathless—when the image of her wolf taking her like an animal made her fantasies run wild. Coitus could be had outside of a bed as well…standing up against a wall, sitting on a bench, crouched in a garden arbor. The possibilities were endless.

Jocelyn peeked over at him. Perhaps even on a *balcony* above hundreds of people.

Oh, dear God, her drawers would be ruined if she continued on this path.

"Why are you here, Westmore?" she asked curtly, trying to distract herself from mounting the man and having her wicked way with him. "Planning to destroy my father?"

If he was surprised that she had recognized him, he did not show it. "Is it that apparent?"

She didn't dare look at him. "This feud is ridiculous."

"Says the pampered princess who has never lost anything of value in her life," came his disparaging whisper.

An outraged Jocelyn nearly looked up then, and only kept her head down by pure force of will. "You know nothing about me, Your Grace. Nothing about this house or my situation, so don't presume to judge me. I cannot control my father's actions—I can only control my own."

Silence grew at the end of her whispered tirade, but then she felt him shift, his knee brushing the back of her gown. "Fair enough. How did you know who I am?"

"You could have chosen a less obvious mask for one," she said tartly. "A wolf, really?"

"What's wrong with a wolf?"

She let out a huff. "You do know that everyone calls you the *Wolf* of Westmore? Prudence started it back when she would regale me of tales of your many conquests, but then it turned into a descriptor of your ruthless nature in business—according to Tybalt anyway."

She felt him stiffen at the mention of their mutual friend, and forced herself not to feel a sour prickle of jealousy at the fact that Westmore had likely returned Prue's tender feelings. Jocelyn didn't know what made her press on... maybe the fact that she could never speak of Prudence to anyone, not even her own family. The name was barred from their household.

"You were her favorite subject," she said, and felt him flinch. "I'm sorry. I just miss her."

The silence grew between them again, heavy and sticky. A shuddering breath filled the small space. "I miss her, too."

"You loved her," she whispered.

"I did." The duke had a compassionate streak beneath all the ruthlessness, she realized. It had to be painful for him to talk about Prudence, and yet he was doing so, and Jocelyn knew it was only for her sake. Or perhaps he needed to talk about her, too.

"She adored you," Jocelyn said, a melancholy lump filling her breast. "Thought the sun rose and fell with you. Sometimes you were all she could talk about. Before…" She trailed off. They both knew what she meant…before Prudence's rapid descent into addiction.

Westmore inhaled and shifted again. "I didn't find out how much trouble she was in until it was much too late. Roth had his own issues with his father, and Prue was alone, the illegitimate daughter of a woman who scorned her and a man who had claimed her as his own, despite her not being of his blood."

Jocelyn's eyes went wide with shock. "She was illegitimate?"

Westmore's jaw clamped shut and went tight as if he'd revealed too much. Out of her peripheral vision, she saw him give a short nod. "It was one of the reasons she declined the way she did, feeling lost and unloved and unworthy. What mother would do that to her own child? I could have been there for her. I *should* have. I could have saved her."

"You can't blame yourself," she whispered.

"I was so consumed by my own vengeance, by my own woes, that was all I could see. And now, I still am. Retribution is all I have. All I will ever have." His tone went dark. "Tyne has to pay for what he did."

Jocelyn shivered at the unguarded wrath in his voice, the primal growl of it so wolf-like, so raw, that her senses screamed for her to flee from danger. But she didn't. She sat there, blanketed in the shared pain that shrouded him.

"What did my father do?" she whispered.

A fist curled against his trouser leg. He was quiet for so long, she feared the duke wouldn't answer, but then he exhaled. "He tossed Prue to the wolves. Exposed she was a by-blow."

His reply hit like lead ballast, ripping through her soft, vulnerable insides. Jocelyn closed her eyes, her palm going to her chest, sorrow followed by pure, white-hot rage. And suddenly, she knew what she had to do.

What she *would* do. For Prudence. For herself.

Maybe even for him.

CHAPTER 8

Christ, he was an imbecile!

What the devil was he doing pouring his secrets out to the offspring of the man he hated most in the world? Yes, she had been Prue's best friend and had loved her, which was the only reason he'd deigned to talk about what would always be a raw memory for him. But what if she ran off and informed her father or her loathsome cousin that he was here?

What then?

"My lady—" he began leaning down to whisper, but to his surprise...to his utter shock, she tilted her head up and kissed him, her lips soft on his and then harder, as if she needed fortification from the unexpected embrace. Without thinking, his lips parted when she licked across the seam of his mouth in a move that was unnervingly familiar.

Wait. He *knew* those lips. That teasing flick against his upper teeth.

The fucking *taste* of her.

What the *devil*?

Wulfric reared back, green eyes boring into him. Those pretty eyes, like bottle-green glass. He'd seen them dilated and molten with pleasure. Blinking in confusion, he studied her face —heart-shaped with that pointy stubborn chin, pert nose that had been hidden behind a lacy mask, lips he'd devoured over and over—it was her! Lady J was Lady *Jocelyn*.

His scarlet vixen.

More like his scarlet *virgin*.

In disbelief, his finger lifted to curl around one auburn strand. Of course, she'd worn a wig, she hadn't wanted to be recognized. She'd claimed to be experienced. He shook his head. No, she said she hadn't done the act many times, and he'd made the foolish leap of assumption as she'd no doubt intended.

Wulfric frowned at her. What was her game? Was this a ploy by Tyne? Had they been playing him like a hand of cards all along?

"All will be well," she whispered calmly, as if she could read the storm of wrath and doubt in his eyes. "Trust me."

"Trust you?" he bit out.

She swallowed. "You'll have what you want, I promise."

"Wait," he said.

But then she stood, drawing the attention of every eye in the ballroom, including her father's, to the small balcony that was lifted above them like a stage. "Lord Perrin," she announced in a clear voice. "I'm afraid I cannot marry you."

The gentleman in question spluttered, his face turning puce. Instead of the ballroom erupting in wild chatter, dead silence fell upon it. Even the music faded away, guests standing in mortified, stunned silence. Wulfric knew it was because everyone in attendance was aware of Tyne's temper. They were all waiting for the other shoe to drop.

The duke's thin face hardened with displeasure. "What is the meaning of this, Jocelyn?"

His daughter quailed, her small body shaking. Good God, she was bloody terrified, Wulfric noted. His brows pulled inward. Of her own father? That chin of hers jerked up, though he swore he saw it wobble, and the tell-tale sheen of moisture in her eyes. "On account that I've already pledged my hand."

That pronouncement started the blather as a wave of scandalized whispers rose to the rafters.

"Stop this farce, or so help me," the Duke of Tyne threatened in a voice that had the blood draining from her face. "Get down from there."

"It's not a farce. I went to an auction at The Silver Scythe." She forged forward, despite the irreparable damage to her own reputation she was intent on causing. "I bid on a prize there for charity." The slightest of smiles curved her quivering mouth. "The Duke of Westmore."

The noise in the ballroom was colossal, even as his own brain struggled to make sense of her confession. What would admitting that achieve?

"Westmore?" her cousin roared. "You vapid,

useless twit. You've ruined yourself. Who will have you now?"

Wulfric didn't know what the lady had intended with her declaration. Perhaps she'd felt that it would give him the satisfaction he craved by denying her father of his prize. It did, but he wanted to be the one to deliver the killing blow.

"I can think of one person," she said, and her words registered like a hammer to an anvil.

Oh, fuck no. The little minx couldn't be thinking of…

Only then Wulfric realized that her shoulders hadn't been shaking with fear at all, they'd been shaking with amusement. Dancing green eyes lit with glee peered down at him. "Don't just kneel there, Your Grace," she said loudly. "Stand and let us announce our betrothal properly, as we came up here to do. Your idea of using this balcony was *so* romantic." A hand went to her breast and he could practically hear the swoons gathering in force below.

"What are you doing?" Wulfric said through clenched teeth as he rose to deafening shouts. He had no eyes for them, however, only the conniving virago at his side, who had trapped him so neatly, he hadn't even realized he was being spun into a clever web.

"Saving you. Saving me."

"What if I don't want you?"

Her eyes narrowed, glancing down to where his arousal was obvious just from the earlier touch of her lips. Her voice was low. "Your cock doesn't seem to think so."

"Luckily, that part of me doesn't rule my decisions."

"Thank me later, then. Vengeance is yours." She took his hand in hers, and gazed up at him with a fake besotted look that had him blinking, before she turned back to their avid audience and her furious father. "His Grace was courting me in secret for months. He asked me to marry him and I said yes. I choose him, Papa."

Wulfric, even in his ire, had to hand it to the little actress. She was magnificent.

"You were promised to Lord Perrin," he seethed. "Do you know what you have done?"

"Won a duke?" she said sweetly. She had him there, by some of the approving nods from the women in the ballroom. His title outranked Perrin's by a mile. It was not only higher, it was much older. And he was rich. The matchmaking mothers had been attempting to tie him down for years. Soon the sniff of scandal around their secret betrothal would fade by nature of what he was...a duke with a grand title and an even grander fortune.

"You won't marry him," Tyne bit out.

She fluttered her eyelashes. "Not even if I am—"

Wulfric cut her off then, knowing exactly where she was going. A secret courting was one thing, announcing sexual congress and possible pregnancy before wedlock was another. He lifted her knuckles and kissed them, drawing cooing noises from the ladies present. He wasn't a demonstrative man, so this performance would convince the hardest of hearts. "Completely, irrevocably in love," he finished for her.

The brightness of her smile took him by force. "Glad you've decided to play," she said out of the side of her mouth.

"This is a game you will lose, *Little Red.*"

A shiver coursed over her, though her eyes sparked with interest at the nickname, considering the nature of his own. "Not if we're in it together."

He scowled. "There is no *us* in this scenario."

"You want to hurt my father? This is the way to do it. Don't pretend for one instant that you're the victim here, Your Grace. What hurts your precious pride is that I've used you for my own ends. Savor the triumph I've handed you. I assure you, if I know my father, it won't last."

JOCELYN DESCENDED the staircase with her reluctant new fiancé in hand. Lady Darcy would be proud of the way she'd cobbled together a series of events that hadn't led to her ruination or unhappiness. Had it? She glanced up at the silent duke at her side, the wolf mask making him seem even more menacing than normal. Or was that her imagination because of what he'd called her? Perrault's *Little Red Riding Hood* was a story about a girl who had been eaten by the big, bad wolf. Would she be?

Like the bone-deep shiver on the balcony, another stole through her. What *would* it be like to be devoured by him? Her body heated at the memory of him sucking her arousal off his fingers. Jocelyn had no idea what he would be like as a husband, though at least she knew they would be compatible in bed.

She wouldn't be thinking of England at all when he was on top of her.

Biting her lip to swallow the half-hysterical laugh that bubbled up into her throat, she shook her head. Instead of a randy goat, she was marrying a dominant wolf. More fool her, if she thought she hadn't gone from the fat straight into the fire.

She accepted the murmured congratulations as they made their way through the ballroom. They weren't in the clear yet. Tybalt looked like he was about to murder someone, and her father did not look any less angry. Nor did the Marquess of Perrin, though he probably couldn't belt a fly in a fight. He looked quite put out, as did her mother, whose disappointment was written all over her face.

"Papa," Jocelyn said with the demurest look she could muster.

"Study," he barked. "Now."

A low, foreboding growl stopped her in her tracks. "Don't speak to her like that."

"How dare you presume to tell me how to talk to my own daughter?" her father barked, stalking a path through the inquisitive guests, followed by Tybalt, her mother, and the Marquess of Perrin.

"Because I'm her future husband."

"We'll see about that."

In the study, her father took his place behind the enormous desk. Westmore had yet to release her hand, and while she knew it probably irked him to touch her thus, Jocelyn was grateful for the solid strength of him. As much as she'd stood up to her father earlier, she was nervous. The Duke of Tyne had never struck his children, but his punishments were creative.

When they were much younger, her middle sister, Juniper, had talked back to the duke and had been locked in her bedchamber for a week with barely any sustenance. Jocelyn and Jacinda had sneaked her food from the kitchens so she wouldn't starve. Later on, Juniper had been prohibited from going to London for an entire Season, because she had refused to wed the man their father had chosen for her. When threatened with missing a second Season and being sent to a nunnery, she had conceded.

Jocelyn, too, had faced the brunt of his temper when he'd forbidden her from seeing Prudence, barring her from leaving the house or her friend being welcomed. It had been his fault Prue had felt so abandoned and gotten so lost. Jocelyn would never forgive her father for that. And now that she knew of the hand he'd had in exposing Prudence's illegitimacy, because of this long-suffering, stupid feud, her heart was brimming with bitterness.

"You won't get a cent from me, if that's what you hope," her father hissed.

"I don't need her dowry," Westmore said.

"I'll disown the chit."

Westmore didn't move a muscle. "And how will that reflect upon you, do you think? Your daughter has made the match of the century."

"With a reprobate!" Tybalt spit out.

"There you are," Westmore said, with a side-long glance to her cousin. "It would not have been the same without some asinine yelping from the ever-faithful hound."

"Name your second," Tybalt shouted. "I'm going to kill you for dishonoring my dear cousin. She was promised to another, to Perrin. Contracts have been signed."

Her father slammed his hand down on his desk. "Enough!"

"Careful, Tyne," Westmore said, not even rising to Tybalt's challenge as if it was beneath him to even respond. "Don't want to lose the only heir you can control, do you? I'd muzzle your dog before he makes any other threats that finds the two of us in a field at dawn."

"Tybalt is not wrong," her father said. "Contracts have already been signed by myself and Perrin."

"But I have not given my consent," Jocelyn said from between clenched teeth. "I won't marry him."

"I'm your father, I decide what's best for you."

"What's best for me?" she burst out. "Or what's best for *you*?"

He glared at her. "Who saw you with West-more at this club? Perhaps we can manage this debacle you've gotten yourself into. No one will dispute my word. Perrin, what say you?"

"I'll take her," the marquess said, with a lascivious look that made bile sour her stomach.

Jocelyn's blood boiled. They were discussing her as if she were a cow to be handed over. She might as well be, for all the say she had in her own future. And if Westmore decided to take the easy way out and walk away, then what choice would she have? He'd taken her virginity, and that in itself was a perverse kind of vengeance. Perhaps that would be enough for him.

And while no one might dispute her father's word to his face, that did not mean she would not be inured from slanderous gossip. They would all speculate as to why the duke would cry off and let her go to someone like Perrin. She choked back a strangled sob. What did the gossip matter anyway? The loathsome marquess intended to force himself on her and keep her as a broodmare in the country somewhere.

"You will have to drag me kicking and screaming to the altar, I swear to you." She turned to her mother. "Do you not have anything to say, Mama? You would let him treat me thus? Marry me to that…man."

"It is your duty," she replied icily. "Perrin is a marquess."

Jocelyn sniffed, desolation welling in her throat at her mama's callous disregard for her feelings. "And it is your duty to protect your daughters! Not worry about whether your next set of jewels will be enough to gain you more influence as the Duchess of Tyne." Her mother glared, but she wasn't finished. "Your daughters' lives mean something. *Should* mean something beyond material possessions. My God, don't you have a heart?"

Her tirade drifted into silence, a single tear tracing down her cheek, even as her mother turned her head away, coldness and disapproval stamped in every line of her. Apparently, she did not, though her mother's heartlessness was something she'd known all along. After all, how could she endure life beside a man like the cold-blooded Duke of Tyne? Like attracted like.

Defeat swamping her, Jocelyn stepped away from Westmore, as if to unconsciously protect herself from his certain rejection. He hadn't wanted her—he'd said so himself up there on the balcony. It made sense that he would cry off, while still savoring the secret victory over his sworn enemy.

She felt his perusal over her person for a charged moment, and braced when his deep voice penetrated every corner of the room. "Lady Jocelyn stays with me."

Jaw agape, Jocelyn peered up at him, but the duke wasn't looking at her.

"Now see here, Westmore," Perrin blustered.

A burning stare silenced the man, before it was directed to her cousin, who paled at what he saw there. "Since you've issued your challenge, my second is the Marquess of Roth or the Duke of Beswick, take your pick."

Jocelyn didn't hear another word as she was ushered from the room in the arms of the duke who, astonishingly, had saved her from a fate worse than death, despite his avowals to the contrary. But blood would still be spilled, and from the victorious look on her father's face, that was *exactly* what he wanted.

CHAPTER 9

"**H**ave you sodding lost your *mind?*"
Roth demanded. "Tell him, Beswick."
The marquess's brother-in-law,
the Duke of Beswick, leaning against the wall
with his arms folded, gave a nod. "Dueling is il-
legal, as you know."

Wulfric sighed. "That fool challenged me,
and demanded satisfaction for dishonoring his
cousin."

"Did you dishonor her?" Roth asked with a
leer.

"What happens at The Silver Scythe stays at
the Scythe, you know this," he replied. "The lady
got what she wanted, and we shall leave it at
that."

A scowling Roth shook his head. "You didn't
have to accept the challenge. Isobel will geld me
if I even *think* about showing up to a dawn duel.
I've learned that it's in my best interests not to
cross that woman for my own wellbeing."

There was a joke in there about being henpecked, but Wulfric was much too agitated at the prospect of taking a man's life for no good reason at all, and not having a trusted second with him. "You know very well I could not decline a challenge against my honor without being called a coward," he said. "Does that mean you won't be there?"

"No, you ass. Of course I will. You're my best mate, even if you make the stupidest decisions known to man, antagonizing that pompous boot-licker, Tybalt Capehart, of all people. The man is a hog-grubber who can't wait to inherit his uncle's estate and be duke."

"You can count on me to be there as well," Beswick said. "No doubt Tyne will try to be untoward, like hire some thug to shoot you from afar if his idiot nephew misses."

Relief sluiced through him. Wulfric wouldn't have wanted to trust his life to a man he couldn't depend on, and both men currently in his study had become more than brothers to him. He wasn't afraid of Tybalt or his uncle, or whether the latter would try something dishonorable. He was more worried about the woman ensconced with the Duchess of Beswick. He let out a breath. "How is she? Lady Jocelyn?"

"She is as well as can be expected," Beswick said. "Astrid says she is shaken and fearful because her cousin is an excellent shot."

Roth raked a hand over his scalp. "Honestly, how did this even happen? I thought you loathed anything to do with the Capeharts. And now you're to be married to one and dueling another. What's next? Holidays in Bath? Cozy family dinners? Wearing matching holiday vests?"

Wulfric ignored the man's caustic tone and debated how much to reveal. He pinched the bridge of his nose and exhaled. "She's Lady J."

Roth blinked. "Wait, Lady J? As in Lady J who bought you for two thousand quid? That Lady J?"

"Two-and-a-half thousand quid, and yes. Stop saying Lady J like it's a scandalous sobriquet."

"Fine." Roth's eyebrow shot skyward. "But for the record, let's not argue trifles, my friend. I'm still the king of the auction hall, remember that before you quibble over five hundred pounds."

"The five thousand that your *wife* bid for you doesn't count."

"And Lady Jocelyn is now your *wife*-to-be."

The Duke of Beswick cleared his throat with a rumble of vexation. "Children, please! Can we focus on the matter at hand instead of how much your pricks are worth? Like the fact that Westmore might get shot, die, and make his future duchess a widow before any vows are said, which means she will be right back in her father's clutches." Wulfric stared at him while Roth did the same, both wearing the same incredulous looks. Beswick spread his palms, his badly scarred face pulling in more of a grimace than a smile. "I'm not saying that you will, just that you *might*. And you may want to think about her in the eventuality that something unfortunate does happen."

Wulfric sobered. Fuck, the duke was right. He'd have to marry Jocelyn to make sure that she was protected from her father's machinations. As a widowed duchess, she would have more independence than she ever would under Tyne's hand. "I don't suppose either of you have an in with the Archbishop of Canterbury for a special license?" he asked.

"The man runs at the sight of me, and for once, it's not because of my face," Beswick muttered. "Considering how dreadfully I harangued him for Roth's after my own marriage license. But I suppose it won't hurt to ask. I'll be three for three."

"Thank you."

"Now what?" Roth asked.

"We go see a bishop about a horse." They both gaped at Beswick. He grinned. "What? Can't a man make a joke?"

"Married life is turning you," Roth said, with a shake of his head. "You've gone from beast to biscuit."

Beswick's lip curled. "Call me 'biscuit' one more time and perhaps we can arrange a duel for you as well."

JOCELYN SQUINTED down at the pressing note the messenger had delivered to the Duke of Beswick's London residence, her stomach swirling with indecision. How had her parents known she was here? Had someone followed her and Westmore the day before? She glanced at the two faces before her. The very kind but no-nonsense Duchess of Beswick, Astrid, who had taken her in, and her sister, Isobel, the disheveled, bright-eyed marchioness stood on either side of her, both somber of countenance.

"I don't like notes," Isobel said with a frown. "It could be a trick."

"This is written in my mama's hand," Jocelyn replied. "It says she's fallen gravely ill with fever. The coach is waiting outside for me."

Astrid let out an apprehensive sigh. "I think you should wait for Thane and Westmore to return."

"What if she's truly feverish?" Her mother might be cold-hearted, but she was the only mother Jocelyn had. She'd never forgive herself if something happened, but she also wasn't completely gullible that this could be a ruse to bring her home. "I have to go. Perhaps I could take one of your footmen with me?"

"I'll go with you," Isobel offered.

Jocelyn shook her head. "No, I'd be beside myself if anything happened to you. They're my parents. As horrid as they've been, I'm not in any danger from them."

Even as she said the words, her belly flipped. She *could* wait for Westmore, but she'd already involved him more than was needed. She'd come this far managing her parents, what was one small visit home if they were lying? She would go, check on her mother, and return. At least, these two women would know where she'd gone. Still, her nerves knotted, indecision plaguing her.

"Then take this," Isobel said, handing her what looked like a very sharp hairpin in the shape of a crimson rose. "Lady Darcy says a woman should always be prepared to defend her dignity and integrity."

"Do you read her?" she asked, and to her surprise, both women burst into laughter. The sisters exchanged a look, and then Isobel canted her head at Astrid, as if giving her permission for something.

"I'll let you in on a little secret," Astrid said. "Izzy is one half of the termagant that is Lady Darcy. The other is Clarissa Bell."

Jocelyn's jaw dropped open. "I did not see that coming."

"My sister is a master of subterfuge as well as the written word," Astrid said, pride in her voice. "Isobel, Lady Darcy, Izzy, Iz…she has many faces."

"Who is Iz?"

"Long story," Isobel said with a cheeky grin. "But I pretended to be a groom to get to know Winter a little better when I first came to London. It all went a bit sideways at first, I won't lie, but I'm working on it. My reformed rakehell is coming nicely to heel."

Jocelyn giggled, her smile growing as she shook her head in mild disbelief that this woman was one of her many heroes. "I have you to thank, then, for giving me the courage I needed to find my feet. For giving so many women the needed advice to be our true, strongest selves."

"I'm glad," Isobel said. Smoothing her skirts, Jocelyn tucked the hairpin into her bun and hugged the two ladies. Isobel gave her an earnest look. "If you're not back here by supper, I'm fetching the Runners and coming to get you."

If she wasn't back by then, Jocelyn had the feeling that something dreadful would have happened, but she didn't voice her qualms. This was London and her *parents*. Besides, there would be servants about and it was broad daylight. When she donned her cloak and walked outside, her father's coach was waiting. If she went home, it wasn't as though the Marquess of Perrin could abscond with her in front of witnesses, snatch her away to some secret place, and force her to marry him.

Then again, her *father* could.

Jocelyn's blood chilled in dismay at the thought. What if that was his plan? Panic riding her hard, her feet stalled on the cobblestones and then she felt a palm on her back. Her heart lifted, thinking it was Westmore, and then crashed when she recognized the dark scowl of her cousin. "Get in," Tybalt whispered in a sinister tone. "Don't make a scene, Jocelyn."

She flinched. "Take your hand off me."

"Oy! She doesn't look like she wants to go with you." Isobel stood at the top of the stairs, like an avenging angel about to swoop down.

Tybalt swore so ferociously that Jocelyn recoiled from the anger in his voice. His fingers slid to his waistcoat, and she quailed when she saw the pistol tucked into his belt. Why would he be carrying a *weapon*? Unless he'd been expecting trouble, or *planning* trouble, and now, Isobel would be caught in the crossfire.

"Don't hurt her," Jocelyn whispered urgently.

"Then get in the coach," he said. "And I won't have to." His voice shook slightly as if the very idea was repulsive to him, and that was the only thing that made her stop from yanking herself free of his grasp. Her cousin might be under her father's thumb, but he wasn't a murderer.

"Fine, Tybalt, I will," she said, and looked over her shoulder, forcing a smile to her face. "All is well, Iz. I'll be back by supper." The lady's eyes widened at the nickname, but it was the only thing Jocelyn could think of in the moment that wouldn't draw Tybalt's suspicion or make him do something stupid. She hoped Isobel was as clever as she seemed.

Once they were inside the coach, her cousin glared balefully at her. "Couldn't you have done what you were told? Don't you know how important this is? We've been chasing Perrin's coattails for years."

"Then *you* marry him," she shot back. "Why do you even have a gun?"

"For protection." Jocelyn blinked at the reply. From Westmore and his friends? None of those men were the dishonorable sort, unless Tybalt had other plans. She frowned at him and he met her expression with no small amount of bitterness. "Looks like you proved me right, that women are only good for one thing."

"At least that was my choice."

His jaw clenched. "So you did lie with him? You selfish girl. You've so very nearly ruined everything, but thankfully, Perrin doesn't care. He just wants you, and so he shall have you. Soon all of this will be water under the bridge." A scathing gaze traced her from head to toe, and Jocelyn's entire body stiffened at the inspection before his words sank in. She had the sudden urge to dive from the moving coach because Tybalt wasn't taking her home. They were leaving London!

"Where are we going?" she asked. "Is Mama even ill?"

"She's well enough."

Of course she was. Deep down, Jocelyn had known that, but as always, her trusting, gullible heart had ever been her downfall. "Tybalt, where are we going?"

His mouth firmed into a flat, stubborn line. "To your husband."

CHAPTER 10

The study was in shambles.

Wulfric had torn it apart with his bare hands the moment he'd returned with the license and seen the ashen look on his butler's face. "Lady Jocelyn is gone, Your Grace, Lady Roth sent a footman with the news. Her cousin collected her. They had a man follow, but he lost them on the way out of London."

The helpless rage had been instantaneous. "*Out* of London?"

He'd wanted to rip that sniveling coward Tybalt to pieces, but he'd settled on inanimate furniture instead. At least for the moment. He panted, sat on a chair, and promptly fell backward because one of its legs was broken. He deserved that. Wulfric hadn't lost his temper in years. Not since he'd found Prue in that hellhole. He rubbed at his chest, not stopping to think what that meant. The two weren't connected. He'd loved Prue. He was...fond of Jocelyn.

Whom was he fooling? It was more than

fondness. Whatever it was, he didn't want to lose it. It felt precious, like the possibility of something more than he could have ever imagined. Hope, maybe, after so many years of feeling nothing. Jocelyn Capehart made him feel alive.

Hell, he never should have left her alone!

Think, Wulfric!

Where could they have gone?

"Hall," he commanded. "Get my pistols and my horse."

"Yes, Your Grace," the butler said, and hurried away.

Wulfric paced the study, avoiding chair legs and broken glass. Tybalt wouldn't take her to Tyne's ancestral seat in Northern England. It was much too far. His uncle likely had properties outside of London, though. But *where*? He needed something to go on, and there was only one place he could get answers.

When his horse was ready, he rode to Tyne's Mayfair residence, calming the rage seething beneath his skin. He was greeted by a butler as he stalked into the empty foyer. Starkly empty. There were no vases of flowers, as there had been for the ball, and he could see servants cleaning and putting dusting cloths over some of the furniture in the adjacent salon. "The Duke of Westmore to see Tyne this instant."

"His Grace is not at home to callers."

"Where is he?" Wulfric demanded.

"The duke and duchess departed this morning for Newcastle-Upon-Tyne, Your

Grace," the butler said, with a fearful look as Wulfric faltered on his feet, fists clenching. Dear God, was he too late? Was Jocelyn with her parents? His brain worked furiously. He could catch up with them, switch out horse teams as often as he had to, but he had to leave *now*.

"You have the look of your mother, boy," a frail voice said, making him spin around on his heels. A tiny birdlike woman he recognized as the Dowager Duchess of Tyne, garbed in black bombazine that swallowed her small frame, peered at him over a pair of spectacles from the top of the staircase.

"Thank you," he said, anxious to leave. "Good day, Your Grace."

"I'm here until the end of the week, not much room in the cramped carriage, you see, for these old bones," she told him conversationally, making her slow way down. "You haven't seen that granddaughter of mine, have you?"

Wulfric froze. "She didn't go with Tyne?"

Green eyes, too much like Jocelyn's, pierced him when she finally reached the bottom. "Shouldn't she be with you? Heard about that hullabaloo during the ball, that my girl got herself leg-shackled to the Wolf of Westmore." The dowager cackled, and Wulfric wondered if her wits were all there. "Takes after me in spirit, she does."

"Do you know where she is, Your Grace?"

The old lady waved an arm. "Somewhere about with that snot-rag of my grand-nephew, I expect. Heard him ranting about duty and property and doing the right thing earlier. That boy wouldn't know the right thing if it bashed him in the *arse*."

If he wasn't so wound up, Wulfric would have laughed. Since Jocelyn hadn't left with her father, then that meant she might still be here, though she was with her cousin, which made things arguably worse. "Did Lord Tybalt say where he was going?"

"No," she said and cocked her head, watching him with those too-familiar green eyes that made his chest twinge. Wulfric's hope faded, but then he gritted his teeth. He'd pay every Runner he had to and cover every route out of London. He'd find her, no matter what it took.

He bowed. "Thank you, Duchess. I bid you a safe journey."

"Do you care for my granddaughter, Westmore?" the old woman asked, squinting at him with an odd look on her face.

Wulfric didn't hesitate. He *did* care. And he wanted more. He wanted a *chance*. "I do."

"Enough to give up this vendetta you have against Tyne?"

That stumped him. Revenge had driven him for so long. Could he give it up for a woman who might not turn out to be whom he hoped? "I don't know."

"Well, at least you are honest," she murmured, a hint of regret crossing her weathered features. "At some point, you will have to decide whether chasing past demons will bring you the same fulfillment that looking to the future will.

She's rather special, you know. My fool son never appreciated it, but Jocelyn's heart is as wide as it is deep."

"I know it is. Good day, Your Grace, and thank you."

She smiled. "You're welcome. Tyne maintains a hunting property in Dartford from my late husband. Check there."

Wulfric froze as his heart leaped behind his ribs. On impulse, he reached up to where she stood on the third step, grasped her hand, and kissed her lined knuckles. "I'll get her and bring her back."

"No, dear boy," she said, patting his cheek. "If you have any sense at all, you'll steal her far away from here."

~

JOCELYN STRUGGLED against the rope binding her hands. How dare Tybalt tie her up? It was a rhetorical question. She knew why. He'd told her, so she couldn't try anything stupid and escape, before leaving her trussed up in the study in her father's hunting lodge. The house was deserted, a thin layer of dust on all the furnishings. No one had been here in months. Her heart quivered...which meant no one would have reason to come find her here either.

Her lips were dry and she longed for a sip of water. Well, thirst or not, she wouldn't make this easy for her dolt of a cousin, and she *would* try to escape while he was gone. Tybalt hadn't tied her feet so she rose unsteadily and attempted to search the room. Surely there had to be a pair of scissors or a knife she could use to cut her bindings? At worst, she could break a vase or lantern and use that.

Jocelyn didn't find a knife or scissors, but she did discover a letter opener in the study drawer. The edges were dull, but it would do. Sitting down so she wouldn't trip and accidentally impale herself, she worked the tool between her fingers and started to saw. It was grueling work. Sweat dripped into her eyes, and she nearly lost her grip on the opener twice before she felt the rope start to fray. Encouraged, she worked harder and then the tie snapped.

Wincing, she rubbed her bruised wrists.

Bindings might be a fun adventure in the bedchamber, according to Lady Darcy, but not by a demented cousin who intended to keep her prisoner before handing her off to that lecher of a marquess. If she didn't find a way out of there soon, she would unquestionably see herself wedded and bedded to Perrin, and she doubted that Isobel's trusty hairpin could thwart two men at once. She tucked the letter opener into her pocket just in case.

As expected, the study door was locked. Damn Tybalt! The windows were old with iron casings and heavy diamond panes, but they were her best bet...at least until she tried them all and the bloody things wouldn't budge. The casements had rusted shut over the last winter. Jocelyn went back to the door and peeked through the keyhole. Curious, no light came through it, which meant the key on the other side was still in there.

Huzzah!

This would be a delicate operation, but her middle sister, Juniper, was particularly skilled at escaping locked bedroom doors and had taught her the trick of it. Tearing a piece of fabric from the hem of her skirts with the help of the letter opener, she slid the fabric under the door just beneath the keyhole. Luckily, there was enough of a gap from the bottom of the door to the wood floor.

Please don't bounce away!

Using the letter opener, she carefully pushed the key out, praying it wouldn't twist in the lock, until she heard it clank heavily down to the floor on the opposite side. Luck seemed to be in her favor. She tugged gently on the swatch of muslin, and lo and behold, the heavy key came with it. Jocelyn let out a relieved breath. Not willing to waste a second, she unlocked the door and grasped the letter opener in one hand and the hairpin in the other. A noise near the kitchen had her spinning, rage sloshing through her veins. Tybalt would get a rude awakening. She'd stab that sneaky cretin right in the crotch.

Holding her breath, she crept to the wainscoting and placed her ear to it. A floorboard creaked to her right, and she nearly leaped out of her skin as a shadow loomed. With a panicked shriek, Jocelyn lifted her weapons, only to be foiled by a tight grip on one wrist that made her drop the letter opener, and crushed by a huge body into the wall. She didn't think. She started to struggle for all she was worth, kicking out and trying to wriggle loose from what felt like an unbreakable hold. Her free hand snaked up with the hairpin in hand, ready to lodge it into the first soft body part she could find.

"Cease, you little hellcat, it's me!"

Heart in her throat, the owner of the voice registered. "Westmore?"

"Yes." A warm, orange-brown gaze peered down at her. "If I release your wrist, will you stab me?"

"Oh, Wulfric!" Loosening her death grip on the hairpin, she flung her arms about his neck. "How did you find me here?"

"Your grandmother led me to you," he said.

She blinked and then tried to calm the tornado of her emotions with deep, even breaths. Not many knew of this lodge, but it had belonged to her grandfather. "Tybalt is somewhere about, and I'm certain he'll have Perrin with him. Perhaps others. He's armed, too. I'm not sure what he intended, but it wasn't good."

"Your cousin has been detained by Beswick and Roth," he told her, gathering her in his arms. "I did not come alone."

"Oh, thank goodness." She bit her lip. "They won't kill him, will they?"

Jocelyn saw the puzzled look on his face—the fact that she cared what happened to her abductor—but the man was still her cousin and her father's heir. "I don't want blood on their hands. Your hands."

"You don't have to worry about that."

His nose bent to drag through the loose curls at her temple, and strangely, she felt a sensual heat lick through her. But then again, that could just be Westmore—proximity to the man made all her senses muddle and modesty fly out the window. He was just being considerate.

When his mouth trailed down to her ear and he bit gently, making her whimper at the slight sting that was countered by a soft, wet suck, she reevaluated that assessment. Considerate rescuers did *not* nibble the earlobes of their charges. Her sense of self-preservation kicked in as his earlier words registered.

"*Do* I have something else to worry about?"

The Duke of Westmore scooped her up. "Yes, me."

By God, if that growled threat didn't set her off. Her nipples went instantly hard, her core liquefying. Heat blasted outward like a wildfire, consuming her thoughts and distilling her need down to one thing: *him.*

"And why is that, Your Grace?" Her voice was so husky she barely recognized it.

"You should have waited before getting into that coach." The duke stalked toward the study she'd just escaped, stopping only to lock the door she'd just unlocked and pocketing the key. Jocelyn gulped. Her frazzled senses warned that her person was in imminent danger, but a wicked thrill coursed through her blood, reveling in the excitement.

"You're not my husband, sir."

His body trembled at the pert intonation of the last word. He set her down in front of the enormous desk. "Not yet," he told her in a gravelly pitch that promised retribution. "But you will belong to me in every way that matters, Jocelyn. This body is precious, and you will not put it in harm's way."

His nose drew a line up her throat and across her jaw, his scent filling up her nostrils, as his big hand grasped her hip. The duke was shaking with suppressed emotion, muscles vibrating into her ribs, and coiled like a creature ready to strike, those tawny orange eyes of his glowing with purpose and dark passion. Jocelyn licked her lips and swallowed. He seemed on edge, holding on to his control by a thread.

The trembling of his thick muscles was warning enough in itself, but she couldn't help her mouth. "I'm not a thing to be owned."

Those lupine eyes flared. "You. Are. Mine."

The possessiveness of those three words echoed in the study, seeping under her skin and into her bones. Then he caught her by both hips and lifted her onto the desk, the hairpin she still held on to clattering to the floor. In mute shock, Jocelyn stared at him as he fisted handfuls of her already ruined muslin skirts and tore them straight up the center to her navel.

Oh. Dear. God.

The duke ran his lips up one knee to the edge

of her drawers. His fingers kneaded a path forward up each leg, squeezing into the meat of her thighs, climbing higher and higher until she was dizzy with lust. Shoving the edge of her chemise up, his breath warmed her center through the narrow opening of her drawers, and when he eased his hands to the damp fabric there, he met her gaze. Slowly, *decisively*, he split her drawers right open, baring her intimate parts to him.

His eyes burned. Jocelyn didn't have time to be embarrassed before he leaned in with a groan and took the flat of his tongue to her heated flesh in one decadent, wanton swipe.

"Fucking delicious," he growled.

When he knelt and flung her legs over his shoulders, Jocelyn dug her nails into the edge of the desk and held on for dear life. Because he didn't just lick her. He *gorged* himself on her. His mouth worked every inch of her folds, nipping, sucking, thrusting. Even his tongue was inside of her! No part of her sex went undiscovered, and when two thick fingers intruded into her needy passage, she flung her head back and nearly suffocated him with the force of the release crashing through her.

Easing out from under her legs, he rose, and she saw her essence glistening on his swollen lips. His hands went to the fastenings at his tented riding breeches, a large wet spot on the buckskin evidence of his own plentiful need. Jocelyn tried to cover herself, only to be stopped by his hand and a noise of displeasure.

"I'm nowhere near done with you, Duchess."

She huffed out a useless breath. "I'm not your…"

Jocelyn had meant to say she wasn't his duchess, but the word stuck in her throat as he pulled himself from his pants and stroked his engorged length from root to tip. A bead of moisture glistened at the tip, making her sex hunger like a beggar awaiting a crust of bread.

"Are you arguing with me, Little Red?" A tremor ran through her at the name. He gave himself another stroke, harder this time, more need seeping out of him. "Because if you continue, I shall have no choice but to fuck the disobedience out of you."

The filthy promise tumbling from his lips was almost as hot as the sight of him stroking into his clenched fist. She *wanted* him to do that very thing—to dominate her into docility. Jocelyn wasn't altogether submissive by nature, but hell if this man didn't make her want to surrender everything to him.

"What if I am?" she managed, knowing she was provoking the beast and willing to take the consequences. Desperate for them, even. His head cocked to one side, lips baring in a predatory smirk, eyes shining with an unholy light.

"Jocelyn."

A clear warning. A last chance.

Here he was, the feared, revered Wolf of Westmore in all his savage, beastly glory.

She let her knees fall apart. "Punish me then."

CHAPTER 11

Wulfric was going to fuck his brazen little vixen until she couldn't speak. *Punish me then.*

He wanted to laugh at her audacity. Trying to exert her will. Christ, but she was made for him. Not just her stunning body, but the intelligent mind, her quick wit, her complete lack of fear...and most of all, her trust in him. Wulfric could see it in her eyes. She trusted him to take her outside her own boundaries...to break her apart and bring her back together.

He placed a hand behind her nape and brought her mouth to his. The kiss was sweet, tender, unlike his earlier filthier vow. As he caressed her mouth, Wulfric wanted her to know what she meant to him, even if he didn't have the words to describe what was blossoming between them. It was destined to be something more, given the chance, and he didn't want to ruin it. Sex was one thing; true intimacy was another.

It required *him* to trust her, too.

She kissed him back, tongue tangling with his and fingers winding into his hair and pulling enough to sting. Wulfric groaned at her willful behavior, his hands going to her bottom and squeezing. The memory of her last punishment had his cock going even harder. Breaking the kiss, Wulfric drew her close to the edge of the desk and rubbed his crown into her dripping center. She moaned and arched her back. Fuck, it felt as though he was coming undone, like all of his skin was going to shed and fall away, leaving nothing behind but raw sensation…and he hadn't even pressed himself into her.

As if she'd read his mind, she reached down between them and notched him to her entrance. Wulfric didn't release her eyes when he eased into her willing depths, the exquisite slide nearly making his knees buckle. He'd promised her a fucking, and it was turning into something entirely different. Something he'd never experienced with any woman. Not that he was complaining. Wulfric was discovering that everything with Lady Jocelyn seemed to become an extraordinary adventure.

An auction had led to the best sexual encounter of his life.

A masquerade had guided him to the one woman meant for him.

A foiled kidnapping had steered him to a connection he never thought he deserved.

Wulfric could only imagine what was next. A life with her, full of joy and unexpected exploits?

He remembered her grandmother's soft words…would he be willing to let sleeping dogs lie for the sake of true happiness? Could he let himself live and be happy? To forget the feud with Tyne?

To *forgive*?

"Where did you go?" Jocelyn whispered, one hand moving to thread through the strands of hair that had fallen onto his brow. The gesture was so affectionate that something inside of him contracted. He remembered asking her the same thing the first time he'd joined with her. Oddly, it felt like they'd come full circle. He'd be a fool to ignore the significance, no matter how small.

"Nowhere. I'm here. With you."

"Then be with me." She pulled his lips to hers and wrapped her legs around his waist as if she felt it, too, both of them shying away from it, as if it was much too precious to touch.

Lovemaking, that was what this was. It wasn't just the sublime friction, the sultry drag of her body as they came together and withdrew in a motion that was as old as time. It was the look in her eyes, the feel of those fingers at his nape, the sensation of fullness and utter completion in his chest. He could make love to her for hours. Love her forever, if he had to.

Give up everything.

The realization scared the shit out of him.

It was too much, *too* fast. Too fucking soon. He needed to be in control…to regain the power he'd somehow misplaced along the way. His mind was whirling. Never had he felt so vulnerable, so *exposed*, and Wulfric wasn't sure he was ready for that.

"Harder," Jocelyn whimpered, her fingernails dragging over his scalp, hips tightening around his in wanton demand.

Sex, he could do. The rest would have to wait.

Wulfric felt her ripple all around him, the pressure of her inner walls gripping him as he stroked deeper, making her thrust upward for friction as her pleasure built. When he pulled from the clasp of her body, she let out a discontented protest, but he only lifted her to flip her around, her torso resting on the surface of the desk.

Palming her hips, he sank back into her warm, wet depths, and they both groaned at the fullness in this new position. He rode her body hard, coming through on his promise until she was a writhing, needy mess in his arms, the only sound in the room were her soft cries of passion, the sound of slapping flesh, and his own grunts.

Pressure built at the base of his spine, signaling that he was close to the precipice, but he wanted her to come again before he peaked. Reaching forward, he eased her upward so that her spine was flush to his chest. Wulfric delved his fingers into her bodice, rolling her taut nipple between his thumb and forefinger, and pinching just hard enough that she hissed before he released the compression.

"So good," she moaned coarsely. "Feels so good."

He was close, too. "I know."

Skating his palm up her throat, he squeezed. Not hard enough to constrict her airway completely, but enough for her body to go rigid.

"Wulfric." The airless sound had the beat of panic.

"Easy, I have you. Trust me."

She relaxed, marginally, though her panting was still frantic. His pelvis continued its onslaught, his thrusts slightly shallower, but hitting that front wall of hers that had her grinding back against him. He slid his other hand down and made a slow circle on the tight bud of nerves when he felt his ballocks tighten, his body surging into hers one last time as his release built like lightning in his veins. Jocelyn screamed, both their hearts thundering as they spun undone.

White light shooting through his vision, Wulfric bent and slanted her chin up to his so he could take her lips in a wet, open-mouthed, all-too-savage kiss, even as the pleasure barreled through his body in heated spurts. He'd swallow every sound, every cry from her. Take her pleasure as though it were his own. A sob broke from her at the intensity of her own orgasm, her walls wringing the last few frenzied pulses from him.

It was only when he'd collapsed against her limp, sated form, still joined with her, Wulfric realized he'd finished inside her.

~

JOCELYN FLOATED SLOWLY BACK DOWN to earth, her body completely spent. She couldn't begin to make sense of what had just happened. Between his dirty, erotic oaths, the multiple, seemingly infinite orgasms she couldn't believe her body was even capable of, and the breath-stealing—*literally!*—dominance, she was in a boneless, utterly mindless state.

After a few minutes, she felt him lever off of her, but was unable to bring herself to move, confident that her rickety knees were in no shape to even support the rest of her. Too much pleasure had rendered them into noodles. Fused to the desk in a limp display and certain that her skirts—what had survived of them from Wulfric's manhandling—were in a tangled mess around her waist, Jocelyn sighed.

"You owe me a dress," she murmured. "And perhaps a new pair of knees."

He chuckled from somewhere behind her, and then she felt a warm hand pass over her posterior. A soft cloth stroked between her legs before her tattered, torn skirts were gently lowered. Wulfric peeled her off the desk and gathered her into his arms. With some mortification, she realized that the cloth he'd used to wipe them both clean had been his cravat.

"I'll get you anything you need," he whispered, pushing the hair out of her face, and kissing her on the lips. It was a soft kiss...a deeply meaningful one that left her mute. One that translated into emotions and words she wasn't sure either of them was ready for.

A beginning in a flashy club, followed by forced engagements, didn't exactly bode well for a happy-ever-after, and people were wont to say words in the heat of the moment that they didn't truly mean. Jocelyn remembered his growled *'you are mine'* and her breath hitched in her throat. How much of that had been because he'd been in the throes of lust? They'd both been. Because after the ordeal of being abducted, coming together had felt like a meshing of bodies and souls, guided by nothing but passion and primitive instincts.

Jocelyn bit her lip and placed a hand on his chest. "Wulfric. What are we doing here?"

A dark eyebrow quirked. "I should think that was obvious."

She blushed. "I meant you and me." Jocelyn released a breath and stepped out of his orbit so that she could pull her thoughts together. To give her hands something to do other than touch him, she reached up to smooth and re-pin the hair that had come loose from its confines, tucking the fallen hairpin back in place. She felt his eyes on her. "What happens now?"

"We will marry as soon as we get back to town," he said. "I managed to obtain a special license, and Beswick will have a vicar ready at his residence upon our return tonight." When she didn't speak, he went on. "Doing it quickly is best, in case Tyne or Tybalt tries something more to get you to wed Perrin again. I wouldn't put it past either of them."

Nor would she. But the reason for her hesitation wasn't the thought of her father, it was because of the man who stood a few feet away. "Why would you do this? I entrapped you."

Narrowed eyes met hers, as if he sensed the note of uncertainty in her voice. "You didn't trap me, Jocelyn. I could have said no."

"Why didn't you? That evening on the balcony?"

"Your reputation would have been torn to shreds had I denied your claim and refuted any agreement between us," he explained. "I couldn't let an innocent girl get demolished by the cruelty of the *ton*. Not again, not on my watch."

The warmth inside of her turned to ice. He meant Prudence. Of course he did.

Jocelyn inhaled, her heart feeling like it was being crushed under a giant weight of bittersweet envy and inexplicable sorrow. "Because you felt obligated to protect me as you could have done with Prudence?"

Confusion lit his expression. "This has nothing to do with her."

"You said yourself that you loved her." Jocelyn swallowed past the lump of pain thickening in her throat. As much as she missed her best friend, she would always be second-best when it came to the Duke of Westmore. It was quite obvious that his heart had been buried with Prudence long ago. "Prue would have married you, if she'd had the chance."

His laughter was low and cold, making her stare at him, despite being cautious in her reply. "No, Jocelyn, she would not have."

"You were in love with her!"

"I loved Prue like a sister," he whispered so softly, she barely heard it, and then dropped a bombshell that she'd never expected in a million years. "My half-sister."

Her mind went blank and sputtered back to life. "*What?*"

"My father broke his marriage vows with Roth's mother and Prue was the result of their indiscretion." Westmore's voice was toneless, that hard, vulturine gaze back in force, and for a moment, she cursed its return. "Tyne found out and exposed him to my mother, and well, I'm sure you know the story of how she found herself sent to Bedlam."

Jocelyn's blood chilled. She did know, but only from second-hand gossip from her sisters. The Dowager Duchess of Westmore had shown up to Tyne Manor screaming bloody murder and had had to be restrained. A stint in Bedlam had been the only way her philandering husband could save face, and the awful scandal had only become worse when the Duke of Westmore had died shortly thereafter. A breath shuddered out of her. Had her father been responsible for that? For the destruction of two lives?

She glanced at Wulfric in horror. *Three* lives. No wonder he was so hell-bent on revenge. His entire world had been shattered in one fell swoop.

"I'm so sorry, Wulfric."

"There's nothing you can do, it's done now," he said and then exhaled, scrubbing a palm over his face. "We need to leave to make it back to Beswick's residence for the vicar. Unless you've changed your mind. I won't force you into wedlock, Jocelyn."

Silence stretched between them, now that the haze of sensuality and desire had dissipated. Now that their very real future hung in the balance. A marriage would tie them together forever in the eyes of the church, the *ton*, their families.

They were from two different worlds…two different *feuding* worlds. Jocelyn had never condoned her father's vendetta against the Banes, never truly understood what drove men to such violent extremes. Whatever the cause of it, that was long forgotten now, but her father's choices were on him, and she could only stand by her own actions.

What if they weren't enough? If *she* wasn't enough? What if Wulfric valued retribution and revenge over anything he might ever feel for her? Jocelyn had to know. She'd much rather face the sword of truth with courage than feel it in her back because she'd been afraid.

"If we do this, will you promise to stop trying to destroy my family?" she asked in a soft whisper.

Wulfric went still. So preternaturally still, not even the air between them moved. It wasn't an ultimatum, but it felt like one. After what seemed like an eternity, Wulfric took the key to the study from his pocket and stared at the whorled metal as if it were some kind of talisman to the answer he was about to give.

Indecision etched his features, a muscle flexing in that hard, uncompromising jaw, those full lips she had felt graze over every inch of her skin pulling into a tight, ruthless line. Her heart sank, along with any hope for them, even before he spoke.

The duke unlocked the door, one hand on the jamb, head bowed. "No," he replied. "I can't promise you that."

CHAPTER 12

Each time Jocelyn thought of Wulfric's parting words, her heart fractured a little more. A lifetime of bitterness and vengeance could not be abandoned so easily, but she had hoped beyond hope that it would. That whatever esteem the duke had held her in might have lessened the ills of the past and been enough to smooth a path forward for the future.

A future *together*, in which he'd choose her.

But he hadn't.

Jocelyn swallowed hard, rubbing a fist over the gnawing ache in her breast that hadn't abated in the past week. There was no visible injury, no mark that she'd been skewered through and through, but it felt like one, all the same. Like he'd reached in and wrenched her heart out while it was still beating and beseeching him to choose compassion instead of anger.

Perhaps they were fated to remain enemies—star-crossed lovers doomed to be kept apart by their own immovable pride. Because that was the problem with unseen wounds…sometimes they never healed. They festered into rot. Into *rage*. Into something that consumed people whole. And now the Duke of Westmore would have the perfect reprisal—an eye for an eye—and the chance to kill her foolhardy cousin in a duel.

Jocelyn let out a frustrated curse.

Tybalt might deserve punishment for his actions, but he did not deserve to die.

Not that Westmore cared. He wouldn't even give up his lifelong grudge for her sake. Though why would he have? His entire family had been destroyed by hers. As the Duke of Tyne's only remaining male heir, Tybalt was the end of the Capehart family line, and his death would be the ultimate *coup de grâce* for a man like Westmore.

A man she'd so very nearly let into her heart.

You're a fool if you think he's not inside already.

Gulping past the ugly knot in her throat, Jocelyn scrubbed hopelessly at her chest again, the hollow twinge there strong enough to make her eyes water. Screwing them shut, she clenched her jaw. She was *done* weeping over him; he had made his choice and it wasn't her. Now she had to focus on keeping her family from falling apart. From allowing her cousin to make a deadly mistake.

Exhaling her fears, Jocelyn narrowed her gaze on Tybalt, who was currently under house arrest at Tyne Manor, which had subsequently been restocked with provisions and staff, considering the abrupt change in plans. The head of the Runners had ordered him to stay put, pending an investigation of matters surrounding his conduct, launched by the influential Dukes of Beswick and Westmore as well as the Marquess of Roth.

Her grandmother had delayed her return as well, thank goodness, because Jocelyn could not deal with her bean-brained jackanapes of a cousin on her own. Tybalt was refusing to admit to any wrongdoing, arguing that it had been her duty to follow through on the agreement with Perrin. Her father would have already completed the three-day journey back to his ancestral seat, but there had been no word from him on what her cousin should do.

In hindsight, her rotten father had probably commanded the kidnapping.

"Tybalt," Jocelyn began. "Why do you want to see this betrothal with Perrin done so badly?"

His mouth pressed into a mulish line. "Tyne wanted the land."

"Why?"

"Because with a larger shipping port, it would give him an edge over Westmore. Everything was dependent upon it. I was the one who sold Perrin on the idea of combining our estates and resources."

Jocelyn blinked, hearing the desolation in his tone. "Tybalt, Papa is not going to think any less of you if he doesn't get this tract of land or a deal with the marquess. You're his heir, and nothing is going to change that."

"You're his *daughter*, of course you would say that."

"A daughter he was willing to trade to a man as old as Grandfather would be, if he were alive," she said, and glanced over at their grandmother. "No offense, Grams."

"None taken," the dowager said with a dramatic shudder. "I wouldn't want to marry that half-dead overgrown toad either, at *my* age. At least your grandfather was sprightly and could take me for a tumble in the sheets once in a while."

"Grams!" Jocelyn spluttered while Tybalt made a gagging noise. She pushed any thought of her grandmother's bedroom capers from her head, *far* away, and focused on her cousin. "It doesn't matter what my father says, Tybalt. You are next in line as the Capehart male heir. That's how primogeniture works. Unless Papa and Mama conceive a male child at this late stage, which is nigh impossible, there is no way for you to lose your position."

Tybalt flinched. "He said he'd disown me if I didn't see it through."

"He can only cut off your fortune, and even so, not any of the entailed properties of the dukedom or the title. There are laws in place to protect against such things. Papa is posturing to get you to do his dirty bidding." She drew in a breath. "Do you even know what caused the feud between the Banes and the Capeharts in the first place?"

Tybalt shook his head. Their grandmother lifted her hand. "I do!"

"Go on, Grams. Enlighten us."

The old dowager grinned. "My great-great-great-grandfather," she began, then stopped and wrinkled her nose. "Maybe one more great or one less, I'm not sure. Well, he was in love with a Capehart and stole her away from an arranged marriage. Took her right on his horse, like the marauding Viking he was, and rode away." Both Jocelyn and Tybalt waited for her to go on, but she winked and spread her hands wide. "That's it."

"That's *it*?" Tybalt echoed.

"There was a land dispute as part of the dowry, and we've squabbled and descended into revenge of the nitwits ever since. I do believe the infamous bard wrote a play about a similar disagreement two centuries ago."

Jocelyn's brows rose at that, but Tybalt frowned. "It's hardly the same."

"Isn't it?" Her grandmother squinted some more, tapping a wrinkled finger against her chin. "Someone died or got killed. Then it was always tit for tat over the many centuries, with no end in sight."

A bright gaze came to rest on Jocelyn, who shrugged. "Don't look at me for answers. Westmore is well within his rights to go ahead with the foolish duel that your grandson here issued. Tybalt has to apologize and call it off."

Her cousin's scowl returned. "He dishonored

you by entertaining your capers, an unmarried daughter of a duke, at a club!"

"Tybalt, for the hundredth time, I went to that club on *my* own, of my own *free* will. That had nothing to do with the Duke of Westmore. Yes, I entered a charity auction for the sake of my long-lost best friend at said club, there's no crime in that." The white lie tasted bitter, but there was no point in admitting that she'd gone to The Silver Scythe for sex. Jocelyn held up a hand when he opened his mouth to quarrel. "And before you start in about my reputation, let me stop you there. I went, knowing all the risks. This is *my* body and I shall wield it how I see fit. Perhaps you should see fit to start doing the same with yours."

He gaped and blinked at her like an owl. "What do you mean?"

"Call off the duel."

"Then I'll be branded a coward."

Jocelyn paced, her tread nearly wearing a hole in the carpet. "Wouldn't you rather stand for something right? This vendetta isn't yours, Tybalt. Isn't *ours*, and yet we're constantly trapped in a cycle of who can outdo the other, who can kill the other. Frankly, I'm sick of it." She blew out a frustrated breath. "My father is wrong. Rise up, Cousin. Don't bend backward for someone who doesn't care if you take a bullet as long as it's to avenge the Capehart name." She moved to stand in front of him. "You deserve better than that."

"Even after all I've done?" Shame crossed his expression. "To you?"

She nodded. "Yes. We all make mistakes in the name of things we cherish and protect, but if we try to make amends, then we've learned something. You accused Westmore of dishonoring me, when there was no dishonor to be had. At least not from him."

Her cousin fidgeted but looked unconvinced. "He used you."

Jocelyn wanted to scream. That was the thing about dogmatism—sometimes a belief sank in so deeply that a person couldn't change or grow even if they wanted to. When fear and hate became innate and taught from a young age, they were insidious, dangerous things. Hard to challenge. Even harder to overcome.

But change started with one person.

Just one.

"I know you'll do the right thing, Tybalt. I believe in you."

WULFRIC BREATHED OUT, the cloud of his breath forming a white mist in the early morning air. The shadows from the trees in Putney Heath made eerie shapes from the changing light, the dew along the grass soaking into the soles of his boots. He rubbed his gloved hands together and attempted to roll the kinks out of his neck. It wasn't ideal to start the day with a duel, but here he was, called out by Tyne's muleheaded nephew.

Jocelyn's cousin.

The thought of her made his chest ache. God, he missed her! Missed that ready smile, her sly humor, that generous heart, and her beautifully responsive body that he couldn't banish from his dreams no matter how hard he tried. She haunted him, day and night. He'd been a fool to let her go, Wulfric realized that now. Everything in the days following had felt hollow, as though life had been reduced to monotone, overcast shades. Jocelyn had brought color and sun into his life, and now that she was gone, it only made what she'd left behind even more stark.

Well, he'd made his bed and someone had to lie in it.

Pathetic and alone.

Christ, he was a sorry sack of shit. Shaking off his maudlin humors, he walked over to where Beswick and Roth stood with the boxes of dueling pistols. "Thank you for doing this," he told them.

Roth raised a hand to his ear. "What? I can't hear you because Isobel chewed my ear off last night. In truth, I'm surprised she hasn't followed by now, and isn't hiding somewhere in the bushes dressed like a bloody groom. I'll be groveling for months because of this."

Beswick rolled his eyes skyward at the marquess's theatrics. "Shall I do my gentlemanly duty and see if young Lord Tybalt will agree to reconciliation?"

"That would imply that I wish to apologize for my perceived dishonor to his cousin," Wulfric said. "He kidnapped Jocelyn and meant to force her to wed that old codger. I should trounce his arse."

Beswick nodded patiently. "Regardless, the code of honor states that the first offense merits the apology, which puts the responsibility squarely on you."

"Then no."

"Are you certain?" the duke asked.

Wulfric bared his teeth. "What would you have me do? Apologize, offer to be switched for an offense I did not commit? Any deflowering was consensual."

Roth, who was watching the verbal swordplay with growing interest, cleared his throat. "So you *did* deflower her?"

"Fuck off, Roth. That's not the point. There was no disgrace, no shame in what we did."

Beswick let out a breath. "That's where you are wrong, my friend. In the eyes of society, you are both unmarried, and regardless of consent, committed a cardinal sin." He lifted a palm at Wulfric's growl. "I didn't say I agree, only what prevailing opinions are with respect to conduct and perceived honor." He lifted a shoulder in a shrug. "If she were your wife or bride-to-be, this would mitigate most of the bad feelings."

"She's neither," Wulfric said, chest going tight. "We've parted ways." It should not have hurt so much to say the words out loud, but it did. He felt it as acutely as though a lead ball had pierced his breast, shot by an unseen assailant. He nearly buckled from the force of it. "Let's get this over with."

They marched over to where Tybalt stood with his second, a scrawny gentleman Wulfric did not recognize. He'd half expected it to be Tyne, even though the duke had gone back north a fortnight ago, but Tyne didn't like to get his hands dirty. He coerced others to do that for him. Case in point, his bullheaded, eager-to-please heir. With a curt nod to his challenger's second, the weapons were checked and chosen, time and paces agreed.

When the signal was given, Wulfric took his pistol, walked until they stood twelve yards apart but he didn't take aim. Even in the low light, he could see that Tybalt was sweating, his face ashen, his own gun lifted and cocked. Tybalt's arm trembled, and Wulfric braced for impact just as a feminine scream tore through the air.

"Tybalt, no!"

Two things happened simultaneously then. Both men jerked in the direction of the voice, but Tybalt's finger was already on the trigger and the sound of a discharged gun blasted into the silence. Wulfric felt the heat of the ball as it tore past him and embedded in a nearby tree, much too close for comfort. Less than a handful of inches to the left and it might have torn through his skull. He watched through his shock as Roth kept Jocelyn back from running farther onto the field, and then turned his attention back to his opponent.

The young man looked fit to piss himself, the spent gun smoking in his fist. From the look on his face, it had been an accidental shot, even a fool could see it. But still, it was within Wulfric's right to take his satisfaction. Should he intend to do the young man harm, he would not miss. At twenty-five paces, he never missed a target and this was half of that. Perhaps a leg shot then. Or a shoulder. *Or* he could eliminate the Tyne ducal line forever.

Wipe them from the history books.

Claim vengeance for his broken mother, lost sister, and dead father.

Find fucking peace.

"Wulfric, please." The whisper was so soft, but he still turned, his eyes meeting wet green ones. "Don't do this."

The air hissed out of his lungs at the sight of Jocelyn. God, she was so beautiful, her sunset-colored hair loose around her shoulders as if she'd just tumbled out of bed, her eyes red-rimmed from weeping. He couldn't bear to think that he'd caused her any kind of pain, and yet he had. He'd ripped her heart out, because he'd been too selfish to see what was the true meaning of life.

Not an empty victory over an enemy.

A life built with someone he…loved.

The burden upon him suddenly felt different. Satisfaction was a strange thing. So was honor. One could be called a coward for not rising to a challenge of a duel to the death, but it was also honorable to do what was right. But would he be satisfied with that?

The answer was clear.

Wulfric took aim, heard the intake of breath as he did so, and fired into the air. When he saw her face, the light in those green, *green* eyes, he felt satisfaction down to the marrow of his bones. And then she was running toward him and crashing into his arms.

"I love you," she muttered into his neck, and burying his face with kisses, uncaring of their audience, not that any of the men were watching them. "You dratted man, scaring the life from me. You could have been shot and then I would have had to resurrect your ghost so I could shoot you myself."

"So bloodthirsty, my Little Red," he murmured, enjoying the deep flush blooming on her cheeks at the wicked nickname. He took her lips in a long, deep kiss, savoring the sweet taste of her and the delicious silkiness of her mouth.

"Were you going to delope from the start?" she asked, when they finally broke for breath.

He didn't want to lie. "I wasn't sure, but then I saw you, and in that moment, everything became so crystal clear—revenge compared to you suddenly seemed as insignificant as a pebble held up to the moon." Wulfric stared down into the eyes of the woman he loved so much it hurt to keep it all inside. "Ask me your question again, my love."

Confusion flitted across her face before understanding dawned. "Will you promise to stop trying to destroy my family?"

"Yes, I promise. I choose you, Jocelyn. I only need *you*. Be my wife, please."

"Oh, Wulfric, of course I will."

"Good." He breathed her in, heart fit to bursting. "I'm glad, and now we can move on to things like your punishment."

Shining eyes flared with desire. "Punishment, Your Grace?"

He tutted, brushing her cold nose with his. "For running willy-nilly onto an open field when two men are about to shoot each other. I warned you about looking after this body. I'd say some atonement for such rash behavior was in order, wouldn't you?"

Rising to her tiptoes, she kissed him and nodded demurely, before clasping her hands behind her back and skipping backward just out of his reach. His eyes narrowed, instincts perking up at the idea of a chase.

"Do you think to run from me, Little Red?"

She grinned and stuck out her pretty pink tongue. "Come and get me, Wolf."

EPILOGUE

Jocelyn was well and truly trussed. Hogtied, as one would say, arms and legs bound behind her, with a cravat over her lips to silence her many whimpers as a powerful, dominant, sinfully wicked duke circled her with a riding crop in one hand and a feather in the other. Her body was awash with a riot of sensations, the alternation of texture enough to make her teeter on the blade-thin edge of pain and pleasure.

For what seemed like an eternity, her husband had seen fit to torment her with various stroking touches. He dragged the tip of the feather up the soles of her bare feet, the light touch only a precursor of what was to come, when the harder edge of the leather followed up one calf and then a quick lash against her bare bottom. She flinched and moaned, heat filling her when two more strokes followed. The flat of the crop slid against the seam between her legs and her entire body shook. It didn't even matter where he touched her anymore. The entire topography of her skin had become a pleasure center, her nerve endings all lit up. *Every* part of her burned.

"Wulfric," she mumbled through the cloth.

Lips chased over her cheek as he released the tie over her mouth. "Yes, Duchess?"

"I need you now. Please."

Jocelyn felt one of the restraints give, but she should have known better. The feather danced down the length of her spine making her back arch, even though her arms ached, hips rising in wanton appeal. He gave it to her, this time the sharp swat of his large hand making her gasp, right before he slid it between her legs to cup her mound in a possessive grip.

"You're not in control here, Little Red."

"I can't take it anymore, I want to come!" She writhed against the mattress, desperate for friction and his fingers to *move*. The blasted rotter wouldn't. Goodness, she was right bloody *there* and he was keeping it from her!

"You come when I tell you to," he whispered in a low commanding voice that urged obedience.

It was true. She did. Jocelyn had no idea how that was humanly possible...for a woman to have an orgasm on command. She'd laughed the first time he told her, saying that bodies didn't work like that. They released when kindled. Once more, her husband had proven her wrong, and now, it seemed she was attuned to him. Devoted to his demands. Compliant to his control. Ever at his complete mercy.

In full trust.

Usually.

Because now, she wanted to kick him, scream at him to touch her for the love of her dwindling sanity. Tantrums didn't work on him either. To punish her, he'd draw out her pleasure so much that she was a sobbing ball of need by the time he gave her what she wanted, so she'd learned to bite her tongue and let him have his way. It wasn't like she didn't enjoy it…delayed gratification was its own brand of erotic torture.

The duke shifted again, blood rushing into her hands as they released and fell limply to her sides. The knots at her ankles were also loosened, but heaven help her, she couldn't move even if she tried. The feeling of blood flooding her arms and legs was almost too much to bear, the sensation stroked along her overstimulated veins and making her whimper with raw arousal.

Wulfric ran a hand down her back and moved to sit between her legs. He parted her knees, lifting her hips over his thighs. Jocelyn could feel him staring at her, exposed as she was, feeling those eyes burning into her, and sensing his utter masculine pride at the sodden mess he'd made of her.

"Fuck, I love when you're this soaked," he growled.

She arched in desperate invitation. "I need you."

With a grunt, he fit himself to her and drove inside in one hard thrust, the scream tearing from her lips as her entire body lit up like the lanterns at Vauxhall. The orgasm that had been hovering just out of her reach detonated as her husband broke the last of the threads holding her together. Jocelyn flew apart, bolts of lightning firing across her insides, bliss pouring through her like an uncontrollable, never-ending wave.

Wulfric kept thrusting, so hard that the bed frame shook, and her body shuddered anew, her brain falling into a welcome darkness of complete, exquisite bliss, even as her pleasure went on and on and on. Dimly, floating somewhere out of her own body, Jocelyn felt his hands tighten on her hips as he found his release, warmth filling her center in a gratifying gush. When his sweaty body collapsed on hers, she purred in cocooned bliss.

"Jocelyn," he purred into her ear. "Am I too heavy?"

"No," she murmured. "I love the feel of you like this."

A gentle hand swept from her shoulder, down her ribs, over her tingling buttocks to mid-thigh before he took them to their sides, warm palms stroking over her flanks in that soothing motion, fingers threading into her damp hair. After a minute, Wulfric left the bed and returned with a cool glass of water that he brought to her lips. Jocelyn drank thirstily.

"More?" he asked, gazing down at her with

so much love, all she wanted was to curl up and bask in it. She shook her head. When he kissed her, drew the sheets over them, and tucked her backwards into the warm curve of his body, murmuring more words of praise, a languorous sigh left her. Her wolf was always so good to her when he took her on these passionate journeys —before, during, and after.

Much the same as he was outside the bed-chamber.

Life as the Duchess of Westmore over the past year had been everything and more she could have expected. They had married. Her parents had shunned her, which came as no surprise to anyone. Tybalt had returned to the proverbial fold, but Jocelyn got the sense that he might have changed. He wasn't the same defer-ential creature he'd been before to her father, which was remarkable in itself. While he was still arrogant as all hell, he didn't cut her in Lon-don, and he was always unfailingly polite to her husband.

A thank-you, perhaps, that Westmore had let him live.

Or perhaps Tybalt was simply growing wiser.

Wulfric, her darling, wicked duke, was her match in every way; intellectually, emotionally, and physically. Especially the last. The man could look at her across a crowded ballroom and her knees would weaken. Finding a de-serted music room or a private arbor had be-come one of their favorite pastimes. Their friends poked fun at them when they disappeared and reappeared with rumpled ballgowns and disheveled hair, but it wasn't as if Beswick and his duchess or Roth and his marchioness didn't do the same—they were just as besotted with each other.

Jocelyn adored their sexual games, but most of all she treasured *this*. When he held her close to him, letting her know every night how very much he loved her.

"Wulfric?" she whispered.

"Yes, my love."

She bit her lip, suddenly nervous at what she had to tell him, though she had no reason to be. "I've missed my monthly courses for two cycles now."

The hand grazing down the side of her ribs stilled and slid around to the soft flatness of her belly. "Are you with child?"

"I think so. I know we haven't discussed children, but is this something you want?"

WULFRIC'S CHEST suddenly felt ten sizes too small, a suspicious prickle stinging behind his eyelids. The idea of her carrying their child filled him with so much joy, he struggled to put his emotions into words. He scooped his hands beneath her and gently turned his wife to face him. "I love you. And I will love him or her with all my heart."

"I'm glad," she whispered.

He lifted his brows and formed a perplexed look. "Why are you so surprised though?"

"What do you mean?"

"With as much unprotected sex as we have been having all over every garden in England, it was bound to happen." His chest puffed. "I am rather virile, and in possession of some excellent, intrepid seed, if I do say so myself. In fact, it should have happened sooner. I shall have to have a stern word to my soldiers."

A huff of laughter left her. "The enormous ego on you."

"Enormous in *all* things, yes." His knuckles grazed over her stomach, marveling at the fact that in a matter of months, her abdomen would be rounded, a tiny person growing inside of her. He gave a chest-beating grin. "Perhaps it will be twins."

"Do they run in your family?" she asked. "They don't in mine."

He shook his head and winked. "No, but super seed…"

"You are nonsensical."

Amused green eyes met his, a reluctant smile tugging at her lips. God, her face was so beloved to him. Each day that went by, he fell in love more deeply. How he had ever existed before she came into his life, Wulfric would never know. She was his whole world—his sun, his moon, all the bright stars in his universe. Her wily old grandmother had been right after all, because loving Jocelyn, and being loved in return by her, was everything he needed.

Until now.

Until there would be a new person to love.

"Definitely twins," he mused. "Maybe even triplets or more."

Her giggles rang out between them. "We are not having a litter, Your Grace, no matter your fearsome nickname. I would be happy with one, as long as he or she is healthy."

Wulfric kissed the happy sounds from her lips. "Me, too." He wasn't done teasing her, however. He loved seeing the adorable flash of annoyance in her eyes when he irritated her on purpose. "Come to think of it, Wolverine is a good strong name."

"I do *not* think so!" she gasped in outrage, and then laughed when she realized he was provoking her. "Tybalt, then."

"Minx!" He tickled her. "We might as well name him after your father."

"Never," she said with a shudder. "I want him to have a name without any of the sins of the past. Any son of ours will forge a new future, a fresh start, free of any feud between our families." Jocelyn met his eyes, her heart in hers. "On the subject of names, I was thinking that if it is a girl, I'd like to name her Prudence, if that's all right with you."

His throat went instantly tight, emotion daggering him. "That's more than all right," he whispered hoarsely.

God, this woman. This beautiful, huge-hearted, incomparable woman. How had he found her? How on earth had a hardnosed, ruthless bastard like him even *won* her heart? Some-times, he wondered if it was a cosmic joke, that fate would steal her away and cackle that she was much too good for the likes of him. Because Jocelyn was, he had no doubt of it.

"Prue would love that," he said softly.

"I think she would, too."

Wulfric drew her close, wrapping his arms around the two most precious things in his life. Their future was bright, and he intended to live up to the greatest gift he'd been given, every single day for the rest of his life. The Duchess of Westmore deserved to be worshipped like the queen she was. He would do everything in his power to make her happy, and that was his solemn, binding vow.

The Wolf of Westmore grinned. Minus a few punishments, of course.

He wasn't *that* tamed.

AUTHOR'S NOTE

Just a quick note of reference regarding the aforementioned "prick glass" in my story. Yes, Dear Reader, the infamous dribble glass from one of Scotland's most notorious Eighteenth Century sex clubs, The Beggar's Benison, was a real thing. In an age when aristocratic gentlemen rebelled against the stringent morals of society and the church, they loved to flaunt their personal and sexual desires in private clubs where anything went. At The Beggar's Benison in Scotland in 1732, members would meet to celebrate all things bawdy and depraved, including art, books, poetry, songs, women, self-stimulation, and yes, sipping from the occasional dribble glass sculpture shaped like the male phallus. Per the Beggar's Benison's records and their initiation motto, *"May Prick and Purse never fail you."*

ABOUT THE AUTHOR

AMALIE HOWARD is a USA Today and Publishers Weekly bestselling novelist of "smart, sexy, deliciously feminist romance." *The Beast of Beswick* was one of Oprah Daily's Top 24 Best Historicals to Read and *Rules for Heiresses* was an Apple Best Books selection. She is also the author of several critically acclaimed, award-winning young adult novels. An AAPI, Caribbean-born writer, her books have received multiple starred reviews and have been featured in Entertainment Weekly, Oprah Daily, and Seventeen Magazine. When she's not writing, she can usually be found reading, being the president of her one-woman Harley Davidson motorcycle club #WriteOrDie, or power-napping. She currently lives in Colorado with her family. Find out more at amaliehoward.com.

ALSO BY AMALIE HOWARD

REGENCY ROGUES
The Beast of Beswick
The Rakehell of Roth

DARING DUKES
The Princess Stakes
Rules for Heiresses
The Duke in Question

THE TAMING OF THE DUKES
Always Be My Duchess
Never Met A Duke Like You